NOT WHAT HE WAS EXPECTING . . .

Clint stopped just short of putting the key in the hotel room door and had a thought. What if he had brought Denise up here, only to find Amanda waiting in his bed?

He put his key in the lock, turned it and entered. He was immediately aware that someone was in the room. A harsh odor of sweat assailed his nostrils, and he reacted immediately, raising his left arm as someone brought something down on him, aiming for his head. Something hard struck his arm, but he ignored the pain. He drew his gun and fired in one motion . . .

THE GUNSMITH

188

THE ORIENT EXPRESS

J. R. ROBERTS

J
JOVE BOOKS, NEW YORK

THE ORIENT EXPRESS

A Jove Book / published by arrangement with
the author

PRINTING HISTORY
Jove edition / August 1997

The Putnam Berkley World Wide Web site address is
http://www.berkley.com

ISBN: 0-515-12133-9

A JOVE BOOK®
Jove Books are published by The Berkley Publishing Group,
200 Madison Avenue, New York, New York 10016.
JOVE and the "J" design are trademarks
belonging to Jove Publications, Inc.

PRINTED IN THE UNITED STATES OF AMERICA

10 9 8 7 6 5 4 3 2 1

THE GUNSMITH

188

THE ORIENT EXPRESS

ONE

It had been a while since Clint had last been to Philadelphia. As he stepped off the train at the 25th Street station a man stepped forward immediately, obviously recognizing him.

"Mr. Adams?"

"That's right."

The man smiled, taking five years off of the thirty years Clint had given him at first glance.

"I'm George, sir. George Bell. Mr. Fortune sent me to pick you up."

Clint was in Philadelphia at the request of his friend Sam Fortune who, for want of a better phrase, was a railroad magnate. They had met years ago on one of Fortune's trains, which Clint had kept from being robbed, and had become friends. It had been roughly two years, though, since he'd last seen the man.

"Is that your only bag?"

Clint looked down at the carpetbag in his hand and said, "This is it."

"Let me take it—"

"I can handle it, Mr. Bell."

Bell pulled his hand back as if burned and said, "Very well. I have a buggy outside."

"Lead the way, Mr. Bell."

"Yessir."

Bell led Clint out of the station to a buggy parked right in front. There was no driver, so Clint assumed Bell himself would be handling that job.

"Hop in the back," Bell said. "I'm to take you directly to your hotel."

"What about Sam?"

"Mr. Fortune would like you to join him for dinner as soon as you're settled," Bell said, picking up the reins of the single horse which was hooked to the buggy. "I'm to wait for you."

"You won't have a long wait," Clint said. "I'm hungry, and curious."

Clint checked into a hotel without noticing what street it was on. After all, he had transportation to and from dinner. He did, however, note the name of the hotel, which was the Independence.

He took his bag to his room and paused just a moment to admire it. Sam Fortune was footing the bill, as he had done with the train ticket, and had put Clint in one of the hotel's best rooms. Whatever Fortune wanted from him must have been a lot for him to go to all this expense.

He left his room and went down to the lobby, where George Bell was waiting.

"Are you ready?" Bell asked.

"I'm ready and hungry."

"How is your room?"

"It's fine."

"Because Mr. Fortune told me if you didn't like your room I was to have it changed."

"The room is just fine, George. Can we go see Sam and eat?"

"Yes, of course," Bell said. "The buggy is outside."

"Good."

As they were walking outside Clint asked, "Where are we eating?"

"One of Mr. Fortune's favorite restaurants."

"I hope they have steaks."

"They are known for their steaks."

"Then let's get there."

Bell drove them to the restaurant. As they entered Clint saw Sam Fortune sitting at a large table in the back, flanked—as usual—by two beautiful women.

One of the women was a big blonde, full-breasted with a slight double chin. This was the way Fortune liked his women. He called them "well-fed."

The other was dark-haired and beautiful, also full-breasted, but her neck and arms were lean and taut. He knew that when the women stood up, the dark-haired one would be taller than the blonde, with long, slender legs and a lovely, lean but round ass. The blonde would have full, meaty thighs and a big butt.

Either woman would have been to Clint's liking, but

Fortune did not have a reputation for sharing.

"Clint!" Fortune called out loudly. "Loud" was a perfect word for Sam Fortune. When he was in a restaurant, everyone knew it.

The place was crowded and most of the customers turned their heads to see who Fortune was calling out to. Clint was sure that most of the people knew who Fortune was, especially if he was a regular at this restaurant. Even if he were not, though, he managed to get into the newspapers with regularity. He was a well-known figure in Philadelphia society, even though he was only a member by virtue of his wealth. In every other way he was definitely not your garden-variety "society" type.

Clint generally liked to keep a low profile when he was in a strange place, but he knew that being the guest of Sam Fortune was going to make that impossible.

Well, at least he hadn't called out his full name. He waved to Sam and started for his table. The man stood up, his girth almost upsetting the table.

"Clint Adams, get your ass over here!" he shouted.

So much for keeping a low profile.

TWO

Clint walked over to Fortune's table, and the man grabbed him in a bear hug, once again almost upsetting the table in the process.

"Goddamn, boy, it's good to see you," Fortune said, pounding Clint on the back.

"Take it easy, Sam."

Fortune was only a few years older than Clint, but he had acquired the habit of referring to Clint as "boy," as if he were years older.

"Sit down, sit down," Fortune said, "meet these lovely ladies. The blonde there is Dolly, and the dark-haired beauty here is Amanda." Fortune winked at Clint. "She's yours."

Now Clint knew for certain that Fortune wanted something from him very badly. The man *never* shared his women.

"I already ordered dinner," Fortune said. "Steaks, right?"

"Right."

At that moment Fortune seemed to notice George Bell standing by the table. The young man seemed to have no idea what to do next.

"Bell, go and sit down and have something to eat. The waiter knows that I'll be paying the bill."

"Uh, sir, my wife will be expecting me—"

"Tell her you had to work," Fortune said. "She'll understand. I need you here to take Mr. Adams back to his hotel when we're finished."

"Sir—"

"Go, George."

"Yes, sir."

As Bell walked away Clint asked, "Why don't you let him go home, Sam, if his wife is waiting for him?"

"The boy works for me, Clint," Fortune said. "I demand loyalty from my people—don't I, ladies?"

"Yes, you do, Sam," Dolly said. Amanda simply nodded. Of the two there seemed to be more intelligence in the eyes of Amanda. Dolly seemed to watch Fortune every moment, as if waiting for a cue. She had pretty eyes, though, a beautiful shade of blue that was so clear it was startling.

Fortune was seated with a woman on either side of him, so Clint was seated across from them.

"Amanda, go over and sit next to Clint."

"All right."

Amanda slid around to a chair next to Clint, close but not touching. He could feel the heat coming from her body.

"Hi," she said.

"Hi."

She had brown eyes, not as startling as Dolly's blue, but beautifully shaped, almost like almonds.

"How about a drink?" Fortune said loudly. "Waiter!"

A waiter appeared immediately, apprehension clear on his face. Clint remembered that Fortune terrified waiters. Even in restaurants where he was a regular, he rarely had the same waiter when he returned. Sometimes they quit, other times they were fired, and most of the time they simply did not want to wait on him.

"Bring a bottle of champagne," Fortune said, "a good bottle."

"And a cold beer," Clint said.

"You heard my friend," Fortune said, "and a cold beer."

"Yes, sir."

"How was your trip?" Fortune asked Clint.

"Uneventful," Clint said. "I assume you're going to tell me why you paid my way here and put me up in a fine hotel?"

"That's business," Fortune said, "that can wait until after dinner. And look at these two women. They're something, aren't they?"

"Yes," Clint said, "they are." And he was sure they were expensive, as well. Sam Fortune always went first-class, whether it came to traveling, hotels . . . or women.

"Ah, here comes dinner," Fortune said, spotting a couple of waiters coming toward the table with steaming plates. "Let's eat first, catch up on things, and pay some attention to these lovely women before we get down to business, all right?''

Clint agreed, because he was hungry, and thirsty.

''Where's that champagne?'' Fortune bellowed, but Clint really only wanted that cold beer.

THREE

They caught up.

Basically, during the two years since they'd last seen each other Fortune had been making more money, and Clint had been trying to avoid more trouble.

"This boy attracts more trouble than anyone I know," Fortune told the two women.

"Really?" Dolly asked. She turned her startling blue eyes on Clint. "Why is that?"

Before Clint could answer, though, Fortune spoke up.

"Don't you know who this boy is?" he asked the girls.

"You said his name," Dolly said, looking embarrassed, "but I can't remember . . ."

"That's all right," Clint said to her.

"Clint Adams," Amanda said.

Clint looked at her.

"I remember names."

"I'm impressed."

She laughed.

"Don't be. It's not a particularly unusual talent, just a useful one."

"And do you know who he is?" Fortune asked.

"She just said his name . . ." Dolly said.

"And you forgot it already, didn't you, my love?" Fortune asked. He slid an arm around her and squeezed her to him. She leaned into him, pressing her impressive breasts against him.

"It doesn't matter who I am, Sam."

"Sure it does—"

"No, Sam," Clint said, giving the man a hard look, "it doesn't."

The champagne was half gone and Clint realized at that moment that Fortune had consumed half of it. He didn't know how much the man had drunk before he got there, but it was pretty obvious that he was intoxicated.

Clint looked across the room at George Bell, who at that moment was looking at his watch again.

"All right, all right," Fortune said, "they don't have to know who you are."

Dolly pouted, to show that she didn't like that.

"I know who he is," Amanda said to Dolly. "I'll tell you later."

"Oh, goody."

"More champagne!" Fortune shouted.

"No more for me, Sam," Clint said. "I've got to get back to my hotel."

"How was your steak?"

"It was great."

"Best steaks in town!"

"I don't doubt it."

"You wanna talk business?" Fortune asked.

"Not while you're drunk, Sam."

"Who says I'm drunk?"

"You are drunk, Sammy," Dolly said.

"I am?" he asked, squinting at her.

"Yes."

He smiled and squeezed her again. This time one large hand palmed one of her big breasts and she squealed.

"Okay, I'm drunk," Fortune said. "Breakfast at your hotel, nine a.m. Okay? We'll talk then."

"Are you going to be there at nine a.m., Sam?"

"I'll be there," Fortune said, "you can bet on it."

"Okay, then. Nine a.m. Let's have poor George take me to the hotel so he can go home to his wife."

"Fine," Fortune said. "Take Amanda with you. She needs a ride."

"I need a ride, too, Sam," Dolly said.

Fortune laughed and squeezed her breast again.

"I'm gonna give you a ride, Dolly," he said, leering at her, "you can bet on it."

"Oh, Sam!"

"Bell! Get over here!" Fortune shouted.

George Bell got to his feet and scurried over to the table.

"Take Mr. Adams back to his hotel," Fortune said, "and take the lady wherever she wants to go."

"Yes, sir."

"And then you can go home to your wife."

"Thank you, sir."

Clint stood up, then pulled Amanda's chair out when she stood.

"Thank you."

"Sam, I'll see you in the morning."

"Nine a.m.," Fortune said, "sharp!"

Clint and Amanda followed Bell across the floor, both ignoring the glares of the other patrons, who had been bothered throughout their meals by Fortune's boisterous attitude.

Outside Bell said, "I'll get the buggy."

While they waited Amanda linked her arm through Clint's.

"You don't mind, do you?"

"Not at all."

"I'm glad you're not like Mr. Fortune."

"No," Clint said. "I'll bet I'm nothing like him."

"I was worried you would be."

"And you're nothing like your friend, Dolly."

"Oh, we're not friends, exactly," Amanda said, "but you're right, we're nothing alike. She does seem to be your friend's type, though, doesn't she?"

"Oh, yes," Clint said, "she's exactly Sam's type."

"And me? Am I your type?"

"You're lovely and intelligent," Clint said. "Seems to me you'd be any man's type."

"That's a sweet thing to say."

Bell drove up with the buggy, and Clint helped Amanda into it, then climbed in himself.

"Where to, Mr. Adams?"

"I want to go back to my hotel, George."

"Yes, sir. And the lady?"

Clint looked at Amanda expectantly.

"I'd like to go to your hotel, too, if you don't object?" she said.

"My hotel?"

She nodded, smiling.

"If it's all right with you."

"It would be fine with me, Amanda, but you don't have to do this," he said. "I'm sure Sam's paid you, but if you want to go home, that's all right, too."

"You don't find me attractive?"

"I find you very attractive."

"Then you just don't want me."

"I would never say that."

"Too tired, then?" she asked, leaning toward him.

He was able to look down her cleavage, and her scent tickled his nostrils. She put her hand on his leg, as well, and felt his body respond.

"George," he said, "just take us both to my hotel . . . fast!"

"Yessir!"

FOUR

When they got to Clint's room Amanda nodded approvingly.

"It's a beautiful room."

"Have you ever been to this hotel before?" he asked.

She turned and smiled at him.

"Oh, yes, I have, Clint," she said. "Does that bother you?"

He smiled back.

"No, it doesn't bother me, Amanda."

"Good," she said, "that's good."

She came to him then, and he took her into his arms. When they kissed her mouth tasted like champagne, and he was sure his did, as well. She felt good in his arms, and the kiss went on for a very long time. When it ended she stepped back and looked at him.

"How is it that you and Mr. Fortune are friends?" she asked. "You're nothing alike."

"Do you mean—"

"No," she said, "I've never been with him. I leave that to Dolly and girls like her. I only came tonight because he assured me that you were different—and you are."

"Amanda—"

"I know who you are," she said. "Unlike Dolly, I read the newspapers."

"Does that bother you?"

"No," she said, "it doesn't bother me at all."

She stepped away from him, reached behind her, and undid her dress. She let it fall to the floor and was completely naked underneath. Her breasts were high and firm, larger than he would have thought when she was dressed. Her nipples were large and dark brown. The rest of her body was sleek and taut, her belly flat, her legs long.

He moved close to her and put his hands on her hips. He kissed her, gently at first, then more insistently. He slid his hands around to the small of her back, then down to her round buttocks. Her hard breasts were pressed tightly to his chest, and he could feel the nipples.

"Your clothes," she said breathlessly when they broke the kiss. "Take off your clothes. I'll wait on the bed."

He watched as she turned down the bed and crawled into it.

"I want to watch you," she said.

"All right."

He undressed under her watchful eye. In the past he had often enjoyed watching women dress and undress in front of him. He found it interesting to be on the other end.

When he was naked he approached the bed. She got to her knees and reached for his rigid penis. She held it in both hands, stroking it, bringing a moan from him when she slid one hand beneath it. She ran one finger along the underside and then cupped his testicles. Finally she gripped it tightly and pulled him onto the bed.

"Lie back," she said.

"No—"

"Yes," she said, pushing him down with surprising strength. "It's like you said earlier, I've been paid, and what I've been paid to do is give you pleasure. That's what I want to do."

"All right," he said, and settled back to enjoy it.

She was intensely good at giving pleasure. She settled onto her belly between his legs and truly seemed to enjoy what she was doing. She continued to stroke him and pump him with her hands and then brought her tongue into play. She licked him lovingly, at the same time sliding her fingers down below his sack, touching him in a particularly sensitive spot which made his hips jerk.

Then she took him into her mouth.

She braced her hands on his thighs and began to ride him with her mouth, sucking him wetly, bringing her mouth all the way down on him so that she accommodated the entire length of him.

"Jesus—" he said, lifting his hips and butt again, but

she used her hand to keep him from finishing too soon, and somehow kept him in her mouth while doing it.

Clint reached the point where he felt as if he would burst, and still she did not allow him to finish.

"You're killing me," he said, his voice tight.

"Well," she said, releasing him from her mouth, "I wouldn't want to do that."

She moved up on him and mounted him, taking him inside her steaming vagina. He took the opportunity to pull her forward so he could lick and suck her nipples while she rode him. She seemed to enjoy it, if she wasn't putting on a performance for him. This was precisely the reason he never paid for sex, himself. When a woman was with him, and she was moaning in pleasure, he wanted to be sure that she was actually enjoying herself.

This time, however, he wasn't paying, since Sam Fortune had taken care of that already. For this reason he decided to simply relax and enjoy it.

He couldn't really relax, though. Amanda was bouncing up and down on him enthusiastically now, her head thrown back so he could see her lovely neck. He reached up and palmed her breasts, finding the nipples distended in a way a woman could not fake. Also, Amanda was flushed and he didn't think she could fake that either.

He slid one hand between them, down to where they were joined, and using his thumb he stroked her, making her catch her breath. She brought her head down and stared at him.

"What are you doing?" she demanded.

He continued to rub with his thumb.

"Giving you pleasure."

"Oooh," she said, her eyes widening, "you sure are—ohhh!"

Suddenly she started to buck on him, and he could hold back no longer. He exploded into her, and fireworks seemed to go off in the room for both of them. . . .

FIVE

Later they lay together on the bed, his arm around her, her head on his chest.

"You know," she said, "normally I'd be gone by now."

"Is that so?"

"Yes," she said. "I did what I was paid to do."

"You mean Sam didn't pay you for the whole night?"

"No."

"He's getting cheap in his old age."

"Would you mind if I stayed anyway?"

"All night?"

She nodded.

"Why?"

"I have the feeling," she said, sliding her hand down to his crotch, "that it would be worth my while."

He smiled and said, "I'll try to make sure of that."

• • •

By morning she was very sure that it had been *well* worth her while.

"That's never happened," she said at one point, panting, "not—not with a customer."

"I'm glad to hear it."

"No, I mean it."

"I believe you, Amanda."

She snuggled against him as the sunlight started to come in through the window.

"How long will you be in town?"

"I really don't know," Clint said. "Sam's brought me here for some reason, but, as you know, we didn't get to it last night."

"Hmm," she said. "Maybe he wants to keep you here for days, or weeks?"

"Would you like that?"

She rubbed her hand over his chest and said, "I'd like that a lot."

"Well," he said, "I guess I'll find out at breakfast, won't I?"

"Maybe you shouldn't show up for breakfast."

"Oh, no? What should I do instead?"

"I know Philadelphia very well," she said. "I could show it to you, and could take days doing it."

"I'd like to do that, Amanda, but Sam's my friend. He brought me here, paid for the room, and I'm going to have to hear him out."

"Oh, I know," she said, sighing, "it was just—it was just wishful thinking."

"I know."

''We have a couple of hours before breakfast, though,'' she said.

He turned toward her and said, ''Let's not waste them, then.''

SIX

When Clint got down to the hotel restaurant he was surprised to see Sam Fortune already there. He had a pot of coffee on the table and a basket of hot biscuits. He had a buttered biscuit in his hand as Clint approached the table.

"You're here," Clint said.

Fortune bit into the biscuit and looked up at Clint.

"Of course I'm here," he said. "I told you I'd be here, didn't I?"

"Yes, you did. Is there still coffee in that pot?" Clint asked, sitting opposite him.

"Help yourself."

Clint righted the upside-down cup on his side of the table and filled it with coffee.

"How was your night?" Fortune asked, snatching another biscuit from the basket.

"It was fine," Clint said, grabbing a biscuit himself. "How about yours?"

"Mine was amazing," Fortune said. "Did you see the body on that Dolly?"

"I saw it."

"It was . . . well, amazing."

"Glad to hear it. Did you order for me?"

"Steak and eggs okay?"

"Fine."

As if on cue the waiter appeared with two plates of steak and eggs and set them down in front of them.

"Okay," Clint said, "what's it all about?"

"What's what all about?" Fortune asked. He stared across at Clint with a huge piece of steak hanging from his fork.

"Why did you bring me here, Sam?"

Fortune frowned.

"Can't that wait until after breakfast?"

"I think we can talk about it during breakfast, Sam."

Fortune stuck the piece of steak into his mouth, chewed thoughtfully, and swallowed before saying, "All right, Clint." He took a swallow of coffee to clear his mouth and then said, "It's about the Orient Express."

Clint stared across the table at his friend for a few moments, wondering if he was supposed to know what he was talking about.

"The . . . what?"

"The Orient Express."

"What is the Orient Express?" Clint asked.

"It's a train."

"Sam," Clint said, "you have lots of trains. You asked me to come all this way about a train?"

"It's not my train."

"Whose train is it?"

"Well," Fortune said, "I'm not really sure. It either belongs to the French or the Turks."

"The . . . what?"

"The Turks," Fortune said. "That's what they call people from Turkey."

"Sam," Clint said, putting his fork down, "what are you talking about?"

"I'm talking about a train called the Orient Express," Fortune said slowly, "that is going to go from Paris to Istanbul."

Clint continued to stare.

"Huh?"

"I've been invited to take that inaugural trip from Paris to Istanbul," Fortune said, "because of my standing in this country when it comes to railroads."

"In this country," Clint said, "you are the railroads."

Sam Fortune owned three railroads. The Eastern Central, the Northern Atlantic, and the newest one, the Central Pacific.

"Are you expanding?" Clint asked. "Going outside the country?"

"No, you don't understand," Fortune said. "This Orient Express is supposed to be revolutionary. They're going to make history and I've been invited to be there."

"That still doesn't explain why you brought me here," Clint said.

"I want you to come with me."

"To Paris?"

He nodded.

"And Istanbul."

"Why?"

"Why not?" Fortune asked. "I don't want to go alone."

"Sam," Clint said, "you never go anywhere alone. If I know you, you'll have an entourage with you, bigger than any Buffalo Bill Cody ever has."

"Cody's just an entertainer," Fortune said. "I'm a millionaire."

"I know."

"Will you come?"

Clint hesitated a moment, then said, "Maybe."

"Maybe . . . what?"

"Maybe, if you tell me the truth about why you want me to come."

"Clint—"

"Come on, Sam," Clint said, "you're going to have to tell me sooner or later."

"Okay," Fortune said. "When I get off that train in Istanbul there are going to be photographers there. I want my picture taken there."

"So?"

Fortune fidgeted uncomfortably.

"There are people who don't want me to get there."

"Why not?"

"It will enhance my reputation."

"So?"

"Well, there are those who don't agree with you, Clint."

"About what?"

"That I am American railroading."

Clint frowned.

"Competitors?"

Fortune nodded.

"And what would they do to keep you from getting there?"

"They'd kill me."

Clint made a face.

"I was afraid you'd say that."

"What do you say, then?" Fortune asked. "Come with me? Make sure I live to have my picture taken?"

"I can't believe somebody would want to kill you to keep you from getting to Istanbul."

"Maybe to keep me from getting to Paris, keep me from getting on that train at all."

"You have men, Sam," Clint said, "detectives, bodyguards—"

"I have good men, Clint," Fortune said, "but they work for me because I pay them. Maybe they'd work for somebody else who would pay them more. You'll keep me alive because we're friends. You won't be bought off."

Clint buttered a biscuit.

"Will you do it?"

"When do you want to leave?"

"Three days," Fortune said. "I'll be ready to leave in three days, and that will get us there in plenty of time—if somebody doesn't kill me first."

"Us."

"What?"

"If somebody doesn't kill us first."

"Is that a yes?" Fortune asked excitedly.

"Yes, Sam."

Fortune reached across the table and grabbed one of Clint's arms.

"Thank you, Clint, thank you. You don't know what this means to me."

"I'm sure you'll let me know," Clint said, "every step of the way."

"Oh, yeah," Fortune said, releasing his friend's arm, "there's one more thing."

"And what's that?"

"If I do get killed, and you don't?"

"Yes?"

"Whoever gets off that train and gets his photograph taken instead of me? That will be the killer."

"I'll remember that," Clint said and popped the biscuit into his mouth.

SEVEN

Clint and Sam Fortune walked out of the hotel dining room together and stopped in the lobby.

"I'll have George Bell come over and find out what you need for the trip," Fortune said. "All the expenses are on me."

"I know," Clint said. "That's how I know how badly you need me."

"How?"

"You're willing to spend all this money on me."

Fortune slapped Clint on the back.

"I knew you were the one man I could count on, Clint," Fortune said. "We're going to make railroad history together."

Clint laughed.

"How are we going to do that, Sam?"

"We'll get our photograph taken when we get off the Orient Express together."

"You can make history, Sam," Clint said, "and I'll keep you alive to do it, but you can do it alone. I'm not interested."

"You are the goddamnedest man I've ever met, Clint Adams," Sam Fortune said. "You know, I could have made you rich ten times in the past two years."

"I don't want to be rich, Sam."

"That's what I mean," Fortune said, flapping his big arms helplessly, "the god*damned*est man!"

Clint laughed at his friend's confusion.

"Make a list of what you need," Fortune said, "and Bell will get it."

"Will George Bell be coming with us?" Clint asked.

"He's my assistant, isn't he?"

"What about his wife?"

"I'm not paying for her to come."

"I mean, will she let him come?"

"That little gal loves money, Clint," Fortune said. "When George tells her that he's either coming with me or getting fired, she'll let him come."

"And how do you know she won't want to come along?" Clint asked.

"What, and leave all her boyfriends behind?"

"You mean she's—"

"George is a cuckold five or six times over, Clint," Fortune said.

"Why don't you tell him?"

"He loves that little gal something fierce," Fortune said. "I do believe if I told the little pip-squeak she was cheating on him he'd take a sock at me. Then I'd either have to fire him, or kill him. No, he'll find out in good time. That gal will slip up sooner or later.''

Suddenly Clint was glad that George was coming along. He liked the young man, and maybe he could find a way to talk some sense into the lad.

He walked Fortune to the front door.

''I'll be back at seven to take you to dinner,'' Fortune said.

''I'll be here.''

''Where's that gal I paid for last night? What was her name? Oh, yeah, Amanda. She still around?''

''She was when I left.''

''She tell you she was for hire?''

''She didn't have to tell me that, Sam.''

''Was she any good?''

''She was better than good. Your money was well spent.''

''I didn't pay for the whole night, you know.''

''I know.''

''Did you?''

''Sam.''

''I know, I know, you don't pay for women,'' Fortune said. ''Why'd she stay, then?''

''Sam . . .''

Fortune stared at him, then chuckled and said, ''The god*damned*est man, yes, you are!''

Clint watched as Fortune walked to a buggy and got into the back. It occurred to him that maybe he should be going with Fortune. Whoever didn't want him to make the trip just might try to keep him from ever leaving Philadelphia. On the other hand, Sam Fortune was known to exaggerate somewhat. Maybe things were not as dire as he made out, but if he was willing to pay Clint's way to Paris, and Istanbul, well, then, he might as well take advantage of his friend's largesse while it was available.

EIGHT

When Clint returned to his room he was surprised to find that Amanda had gone. She did leave a note, though. It said: "Went to pretty myself up. Dinner tonight? If the answer's no, don't meet me in the lobby at eight."

Was the answer going to be no? If it was he was going to have to have George meet her and tell her why.

Clint walked to the window and looked down on the street below. He'd been to Europe once, to England for a gun expo. He had ended up catching a killer. He hadn't been back since, but he'd always wanted to see Paris. He'd heard that the women there were beautiful. The French women he'd met in this country had lived up to their billing. He was anxious to see if most of them did.

With nothing to do until Bell arrived he pulled off his boots, reclined on the bed with his gun close at hand, and fell asleep.

• • •

Baker Jack knocked on the office door of his boss and entered without waiting to be told to. It was a small thing, but it annoyed his boss and Baker needed that. He knew he was chained to the money, but he tried to annoy the man in little ways.

"Goddamn it, can't you wait!" the man behind the desk shouted.

He'd jumped to his feet as Baker entered, and was hastily doing up his pants. His secretary, the lovely Miss Diane—her last name, not her first—came out from beneath the desk and hurried past Jack to the outer office. He had always felt that she was a kindred spirit, since they both had first names for last names. Maybe their parents had had the same sense of humor.

"Uh, sorry, Boss," he said. "I didn't know you were busy."

"Goddamn fool!" the other man said, seating himself behind his desk now that his pants were fastened. "If I didn't need you I'd fire your ass."

"Yes, sir." Jack called the older man "sir" when he knew it would annoy him, like now.

"Don't 'sir' me, damn it!" the man said. "That just adds insult to injury. Did you follow him?"

"Yes."

"What happened?"

"He had dinner with a man who came in on a train yesterday."

"Who is he?"

"I checked with the hotel," Jack said. "His name's Clint Adams."

"Fuck!" the other man snapped. "I knew it!"

"You knew he'd bring in Adams?"

"Why do you think I need you, Jack?" the man asked. "Do you know if Adams is going to accompany him on the trip?"

"I couldn't get that close."

"All right," the man said. "Follow Bell."

"That little twerp?" Jack asked. "What for?"

"Because if Sam is going to take Adams with him, he'll send Bell over to fetch for him. Watch Bell. If he goes shopping for Adams, that means the Gunsmith is going to Paris with Fortune—and then he's yours, if you think you can handle him."

"I can handle anybody," Baker Jack said.

His boss smiled and said, "That's what I wanted to hear. Now get out of here . . . and send Miss Diane back in. We didn't finish our, uh, dictation."

Clint was awakened by a timid knocking at the door. Perhaps it had even been going on for a while. He got up and walked to the door with his gun in his hand. When he opened the door George Bell jumped back in fright.

"Jesus!" he said. "Do you n-need that gun?"

"Not for you, George," Clint said, putting the gun behind his back. "You're my friend."

"Yes, sir, I—I am."

"But it might not have been you," he went on, "and then I might have needed it."

"Really?"

"Yes, really."

"What a frightening way to live."

"Come on in, George."

Bell entered the room and Clint closed the door. He walked to the bed and holstered the gun.

"Mr. Fortune says you're going to Europe with us," Bell said.

"That's right."

"I'm to get you what you need."

"I didn't make a list yet," Clint said. "Have a seat. It won't be a long one."

"Yes, sir."

Clint sat at a writing desk against the wall and started to make a short list, mostly clothing.

"You're going on the trip, then?" he asked Bell.

"Yes, sir."

"No trouble with, uh, your wife?"

"She won't be happy," Bell said, "but she knows that I have to do my job."

"She's a good wife, then?"

"Oh, yes, sir," Bell said, "she's a very good wife. I couldn't ask for better."

"How long have you been married?"

"About two years, sir."

Clint wondered if she had been cheating all that time. From Fortune's attitude, he guessed that she probably had.

Poor kid.

Clint finished his list and stood up, carried it to Bell, who was standing by the door.

"Here you go. I've got my sizes on there."

"I'll take care of it, sir," Bell said, accepting the list.

"Do you have enough money?"

Bell smiled.

"I'll be charging it to Mr. Fortune, sir."

"Good," Clint said, "then get yourself some new clothes."

"Oh, sir, I couldn't do that."

"Sam said I could have anything I wanted, right?"

"Well, yes, sir, but—"

"Then I want you to get some new clothes, George," Clint said. He placed his hand on the younger man's shoulder. "Don't argue with me."

"No, sir."

"Good," Clint said, "and bring them back here with my stuff. We'll hide it from him until we're on the ship."

"Oh," Bell said, "ship . . ."

"What's wrong?"

"I've, uh, never been on a ship, sir," Bell said, "or a boat of any kind."

"Are you afraid you'll get sick?"

"Yes, sir, I am."

"You won't."

"I won't?"

"No," Clint said. "Take my word for it. We'll take care of it."

Bell looked genuinely grateful.

"Thank you, sir."

"That's all right."

Bell turned to open the door.

"And, George?"

"Yes, sir?"

"Don't call me 'sir' all the time. My name's Clint."

"Yes, sir, uh, I mean, Clint. Yes, si—uh—"

"We'll work on it," Clint said. "You go ahead and do that shopping."

"I will, si—uh, I will, Clint. I'll be back in no time."

"Just be back by six," Clint said, "otherwise take your time."

Bell nodded and went out the door.

NINE

Baker Jack followed the twerp, Bell, from store to store. It was obvious that he wasn't shopping for himself, but for the Gunsmith. That meant that Adams was definitely going with Fortune on the trip. Jack followed Bell until he got back to Adams's hotel, then broke off the tail and went to tell his boss the news he knew would annoy him.

His boss hated complications.

When George Bell returned to the room at five p.m. with his purchases, Clint made him show him what he had bought for himself.

"Two suits," Bell said. "I didn't dare buy any more."

One was black and the other gray.

"You have better taste in clothes than I have,

George," Clint said, meaning it. "What did you get for me?"

"What you asked for, but the shirts are not as plain . . . here, I'll show you. . . ."

As it turned out Bell had done a better job shopping for Clint than he ever could have done himself. The clothes he'd bought would fit in perfectly in Europe.

"What are you doing for dinner, George?" Clint asked, after he had stowed the clothing away.

"Just going home."

"Would you like to join me and Sam tonight?"

Bell actually backed up a step.

"Oh, I couldn't . . ."

"George, are you afraid of Sam Fortune?"

"Yes," Bell said without hesitation. "Everyone I know is . . . except you."

"That's because Sam and I are friends."

"Well, I can tell you, Mr. Adams, from personal observation, Mr. Fortune doesn't have many friends."

"What's he told you about this trip?"

"That he's going to make history . . . if he lives through it."

"Oh, he'll live through it," Clint said. "That's what I'm going along to make sure of."

"Could you do me a favor, Mr. Adams?"

"I will if you call me Clint."

"All right, Clint."

"What's the favor?"

Bell took a deep breath and said, "Could you manage to keep me alive, as well?"

Clint laughed and clapped the young man on the shoulder.

"I'll see if I can fit that in, George."

• • •

"It's obvious that Fortune has hired himself a gunman to be his bodyguard."

Jack didn't say anything, just stood there and enjoyed his boss's discomfort.

"This man, Adams, has a huge reputation, Baker," the man said. "Are you going to be able to handle him?"

"Nobody lives up to a reputation, Boss," Jack said. "Besides, his reputation was made in the West, not here in the East among intelligent people."

"Like you?" his boss asked. "Intelligent people who use guns?"

"Yes," Baker Jack said, "exactly like me."

"Well, then," the other man said, sitting back in his chair, "the only question remains whether to take care of them here, or abroad."

"That will be up to you," Jack said. "You're the boss."

"I'm glad you remember that, Baker," the other man said. "Sometimes I think you forget."

Baker Jack smiled.

"I never forget who has the money."

Baker Jack's boss gave him a long look and said, "Find out when they're leaving and then I'll decide what we should do."

"I'll get right on it."

After Baker Jack left, the man behind the desk stared at the door for a while. He was of two minds about his employee. He did not like the man's arrogance, and yet

Jack got done every job he was given. You didn't find men like that very often.

Maybe he'd have to make a decision about Baker Jack after this whole Orient Express business was taken care of.

TEN

Clint met Sam Fortune in the lobby at six. For a change Fortune was alone and did not have a woman on each arm.

"Ready for dinner?"

"I just have to leave a message at the desk," Clint said.

"For whom?"

"Amanda."

"That's not very gentlemanly."

"What?"

"Well, she'll get all dressed up and come all the way over here only to find a message at the desk."

"What do you suggest I do?"

"Send a message to her."

"I don't know how to get in touch with her."

"I do," Fortune said. "You forget I'm the one who hired her."

"You're right," Clint said, "I am forgetting. Okay, I'll write a message and send it."

"I'll have the hotel send it."

"Do they do that?"

Fortune smiled.

"They'll do it for me."

They walked to the desk, where Clint requested pencil and paper and got it. He wrote Amanda a note, saying that he didn't know when he'd be back and that he could probably see her tomorrow. Fortune then made arrangements to have the message delivered.

"All right," he said, turning away from the desk, "now that's taken care of we can go eat."

"There's one more thing."

"What's that?"

"George Bell."

"What about him?"

"Let's go and pick him up and take him to dinner with us."

"Whatever for?" Fortune asked, looking surprised.

"He's going to be going with us, isn't he?"

"Yes."

"Well, I kind of like him and I'd like to get to know him better."

"Why?" Fortune asked, still puzzled. "He *works* for me. You want me to eat with him?"

"When did you become such a snob?"

"Me? I've always been a snob. This is nothing new."

"Well, do it as a favor to me, then."

"Okay, okay," Fortune said. "We'll go get Bell."

"And his wife."

"What? That shrew?"

"I'd like to meet her."

"You wouldn't be thinking about fixing young Bell's marriage, would you?"

"I'd just like to meet her, Sam."

"She's a pretty little thing," Fortune said warningly, "and she's got fire. To tell you the truth, I don't know what she sees in Bell."

"Was he working for you when he got married?"

"As a matter of fact, he had just started working for me. Oh, I see. You think she married him for *my* money?"

"What do you think?"

"I think it's very possible. You know, now that I think about it, this might be fun."

George Bell was the most surprised young man in the world when Clint and Fortune showed up on his doorstep and invited him to dinner.

Standing in the doorway he said, "I can't, sir. I already told Denise I'd be eating at home."

"Well, bring her with you, man," Fortune said magnanimously. "How often does she get to go out to dinner?"

"Well . . . hardly ever."

"She'll jump at the chance."

"Yes, sir," Bell said, "I believe she will. All right, I'll . . . I'll ask her."

"Don't ask, lad," Fortune said with a wink, "tell!"

"Yes, sir."

"We'll wait in the carriage."

Once he'd agreed to take George and Denise Bell with them to dinner, they had switched from the smaller buggy to the large carriage.

"Watch this," Fortune said as they walked to the carriage, "the arrogant little bitch will say no."

They were sitting in the carriage when George Bell came out.

"Well?" Fortune asked.

"Well, sir," Bell said, "she, uh, said she'd be delighted, but she needed some time to get ready."

"Time? How much time?"

"Well, sir, she generally takes, uh—"

"Never mind, Bell," Fortune said. "Come in here and sit down, and we'll all wait together while your wife pretties herself up."

"Thank you, sir."

Bell got in and sat across from Clint and Fortune.

"It'll be worth the wait, sir," Bell said. "I can guarantee that."

"We'll see about that, won't we?" Fortune said.

"Yes, sir. It was really very nice of you to, uh, invite us to dinner, sir."

"Yes, yes," Fortune said. "I just thought since we'll be traveling together you and Clint should get to know each other."

Bell exchanged a glance with Clint that said they already had a secret they were keeping from Fortune, namely the clothes Bell had bought himself.

"That will be nice, sir," Bell said.

ELEVEN

They waited a little over an hour and just when Fortune was getting impatient the door to the house opened and Denise Bell came out.

Clint was stunned. She was wearing a long dress cut very low to show most of her breasts, which were like swollen grapefruits. Even Fortune, who had seen her before, was surprised. By the time she reached the carriage all three men had gotten out.

"Denise, you remember my boss, Mr. Fortune?" George Bell said.

"Of course," she said, smiling sweetly, "he's the reason you keep coming home late at night. Mr. Fortune?" She extended her hand.

"Call me Sam," Fortune said, taking her hand and kissing it.

"Uh, and this is Clint Adams, a friend of Mr. Fortune's."

"Mr. Adams," she said, extending her hand, "George has talked about you quite a bit."

"He has?" Fortune asked, looking puzzled.

Clint took Denise's hand and held it briefly.

"It's a pleasure to meet you," he said, but he didn't feel that way. Now that he saw her he had no doubt that Fortune was right; she was cheating on poor young Bell every chance she got. She had the hottest eyes he'd ever encountered on a woman, and right now they were fixed on him.

He *was* surprised at one thing, though. Denise Bell had to be at least six or eight years older than her husband, which put her in her early thirties.

"Why don't we all go to dinner somewhere where it's light enough to see this lovely creature?" Fortune said.

"Mr. Fortune," Denise said, "Sam, you sure know what to say, don't you?"

Fortune put his hand out to assist her into the carriage and then got in right after her.

Clint and Bell exchanged a glance and then followed them in.

Fortune took them to a large, well-lighted, expensive restaurant that had a huge entry lobby where they were met by a maître d' who made a fuss over him. Fortune made sure that Denise Bell was sitting next to him. On her other side was her husband, and across from her sat Clint.

Clint did not have a chance to talk to Fortune in private, which he desperately wanted to do. He knew his friend enough to know that he was smitten with Denise Bell and her grapefruit-sized breasts. This was trouble George Bell didn't need, and Clint felt like he was the one who'd instigated it.

"Let's have a bottle of champagne," Fortune said. He looked at Denise and asked, "Would you like that, my dear?"

"I would love that, Sam."

"Sam," Clint said, "I'm sorry, but I forgot there's something I need to talk about."

"Now? Can't it wait?"

"No," Clint said, "it can't wait. Just take a walk with me for a minute."

"Would you excuse me, my dear?" Fortune said to Denise.

"Of course, Sam."

Fortune and Clint stood up and walked out into the restaurant's lobby.

"What is it?" Fortune asked.

"Are you crazy?" Clint asked. "What do you think you're doing?"

"What are you talking about?"

"This is a married woman, Sam," Clint said, "and she's here with her husband, who happens to work for you."

"Clint," Fortune said, "did you see this woman's body? She's got—"

"She's married to Bell!"

"And how do you figure that? I've met her before but never saw her dressed up. Where does he get off marrying a woman who looks like that? She's—"

" 'Married' is the key word here, Sam," Clint said. "She and Bell are married, and he's going to Europe with us."

"What are you trying to say?"

"I'm trying to say get your head out of your crotch, Sam," Clint said. "There are a lot of women in the world. You can't have this one."

Fortune seemed to think about what Clint was saying, and then started to nod.

"Okay," Fortune said, "okay, you're right. I got carried away when I saw her."

"I noticed."

"I saw you looking at her, too."

"Looking," Clint said, "all I was doing was looking."

"Okay," Fortune said, "look, when we get back inside you sit in my seat and I'll sit in yours."

"Wait a minute—"

"We've got to do it that way," Fortune said. "You know me, when a woman like that gets close to me . . ."

"All right, all right," Clint said, "I'll sit next to her—but talk to Bell a little, huh? Make him feel like part of the team."

"What team?" Fortune asked.

"Us," Clint said, "the three of us, we're going to be a team on this trip."

"I've never been a team."

Clint patted Fortune on the back and said, "You'll like it."

TWELVE

They went back into the dining room and exchanged seats. Both George and Denise Bell gave them a strange look as they seated themselves.

"Well, young George, tell me how you feel about this trip to Paris."

"I'll tell you how *I* feel, Sam," Denise said. "I don't think you should be taking George away from me, whisking him off to Paris."

"It's my job, Denise."

"I know it is, George," Denise said, "which is why I'm not standing in your way, but I still don't think it's right. What does your wife think about you going off without her, Sam?"

"I'm not married, Denise," Fortune said, "so I don't have to worry about that."

"And you?" she asked Clint. "Are you leaving some poor woman behind?"

"Not one woman," Clint said, "many women."

Denise stared at him with those hot eyes and then said, "You know what? I believe you."

The waiter came over and Fortune said, "Why don't I just order for everyone, since I come here all the time."

"That's an excellent idea," Denise said, "order for all of us, Sam."

Clint and Bell agreed, and Fortune ordered steak dinners for everyone.

"And bring a bottle of champagne before dinner," Fortune told the waiter.

"Yes, sir."

Fortune turned to Bell and said, "Let's talk a little about this trip."

"Why are you going on this trip?" Denise asked Clint while Fortune and Bell talked.

"Why not?"

"You don't work for Sam Fortune."

"No, I don't," Clint said. "I'm his friend and he invited me."

"I think it's silly," she said. "Going all the way to Paris to take a train to . . . to God knows where."

"Istanbul."

"Wherever that is."

"You mean you wouldn't like to go to Paris?" Clint asked.

"No, why would I? I belong here, in the United States. There's enough to keep me busy here."

Clint studied Denise's face and figured that she was

about thirty, probably no more, maybe a little less. In the dark he'd guessed her older, but he thought that was because she seemed mature—certainly too mature for George Bell.

"You've probably been from one end of this country to the other, haven't you?" she asked.

"I guess I have."

"Been anywhere else?"

Clint found it difficult to have a conversation with her without having his eyes drift down to her cleavage. He thought it was a damned good idea that he changed seats with Sam Fortune. He'd seen his friend fall in love with a woman for a lot less—a *lot* less.

"I've been to England," he said, "and South America—and I went to Australia once."

"Australia," she said. "I'm not even sure I know where that is."

By the time he finished telling her where it was and what it was like the champagne had arrived. The waiter popped the cork and poured them each a glass.

"Here's to our trip," Fortune said, raising his glass.

"To the trip," Clint said.

Bell repeated it, and then they all looked at Denise Bell.

"Oh, all right," she said, "you've got me outnumbered. Here's to your trip."

As they raised their glasses and drank, Clint felt something on his leg and realized it was Denise Bell's bare foot.

THIRTEEN

The steaks were tender, the wine Fortune ordered was excellent, and Denise Bell's foot kept moving up and down Clint's leg all during dinner. Her hot eyes kept burning into him, and he knew why she had so many lovers. How many men could resist the combined efforts of those eyes and her breasts?

"When will you be leaving?" Denise asked him.

"In a day or two," Clint said. "I'm not sure. It's up to Sam."

"Maybe I'll get to see you again before then."

He smiled and said, "I doubt it, Denise."

She laughed and slid her toes underneath the leg of his trousers.

"I think I will," she said.

Clint thought it was time to join Bell and Fortune's conversation.

• • •

Clint tried to pay attention to what Fortune and Bell were talking about, but sitting next to Denise Bell made it difficult. When dinner was over he was the first one to stand up and get away from Denise's groping foot.

"Well, Mr. Fortune," George Bell said, also standing, "this was all, uh, very nice."

Clint couldn't blame Bell for being very puzzled about what had happened that night. As far as Clint was concerned, nothing had turned out as he had hoped. Although Fortune had kept up a conversation with Bell through most of dinner, Clint could tell that it was forced. Fortune truly didn't see how anyone he employed could have anything important to say to him if it didn't involve work—and even then he didn't put much credence in what other people said. That was why he was such a success. Clint told himself he should have realized that to begin with. Whatever Sam Fortune was doing, however he was doing it, he was obviously doing something right.

Denise stood and her husband helped her on with her wrap. She arranged it so that while her shoulders were covered, her cleavage was still very much in view.

"I'll get the carriage," Bell said.

"And I'll take care of the bill," Fortune said.

"You can keep me company in the lobby, Clint," Denise said, and before he could protest she slipped her arm through his.

They walked to the lobby with her husband, then waited there while he went outside.

"You're a very interesting man, Clint," she said.

"And I have the feeling you're a very bad wife, Denise."

Instead of being insulted, she laughed.

"I'm not, actually," she said. "I'm really a very good wife—but I'm a bad lover. Actually, it's George who's a bad lover—inexperienced, really. But while he's learning I'm having to find my . . . satisfaction elsewhere."

"And when George is able to satisfy you, will you stop looking elsewhere?"

"But of course," she said, "but that won't be for a long time."

"Maybe you should step up his lessons."

"That would confuse the poor boy," she said. "He's a very slow learner."

"And what will you be doing while he's in Europe?"

"I think the question should be what will you be doing later tonight?" she asked, squeezing his arm to her breast. "I can get out."

"How?"

"George believes whatever I tell him."

"Well, I'm sorry," Clint said, "but I'm not available."

"Too bad," she said, contriving to look sad. "I guess I'll have to look for my satisfaction somewhere else tonight."

"I guess so."

She smiled at him and said, "I'll bet Sam would be interested."

"You wouldn't."

She smiled, and Clint knew that if she threw herself at Fortune the man wouldn't be able to help himself.

"All right," he said.

"All right, what?"

"I'll meet you later."

"Wonderful," she said. "Where?"

"At my hotel, the Independence."

"Charming," she said. "They have wonderful rooms there."

As George Bell came back into the building and Fortune rejoined them from the dining room, Clint didn't even wonder how she knew that.

They dropped George and Denise Bell off at their residence first.

"Sam," Denise said, "dinner was marvelous. Thank you."

She leaned forward in the carriage to kiss his cheek, and her breasts almost spilled from her dress at the same time Fortune almost fell into her cleavage. Clint knew he was right. Fortune would never have been able to resist her.

"Thanks a lot, Mr. Fortune," Bell said, shaking his boss's hand.

"It was my pleasure, George."

Bell stepped out first and then helped Denise from the carriage.

"Denise, darling," he said to her, "you forgot to say good-bye to Clint."

"Oh, silly me," she said. She extended her hand and Clint shook it. "Good night, Mr. Adams."

"Good night, Mrs. Bell."

"Night, Clint. See you tomorrow."

"Be in the office early, George," Fortune said. "We have arrangements to make."

"Yes, sir," Bell said, "bright and early."

As Bell and his wife moved out of earshot, Fortune asked Clint, "What the hell is going on?"

"What do you mean?"

"I mean you and Mrs. Bell."

"I've got calluses on my shin from where her bare foot was rubbing all night."

"See? Didn't I tell you? She plays around, and I don't wonder why. There's no way Bell can be satisfying a woman like that—in or out of bed!"

"Just don't get any ideas, Sam," Clint said. "You'll just start trouble."

"You tell me how a man can look at a woman like that and not get ideas."

As Fortune pounded on the roof of the carriage for the driver to move on, Clint thought, How, indeed?

FOURTEEN

When Clint returned to his hotel there was a message waiting for him at the desk. It was from Amanda, telling him that she was available as late as he wanted her. Clint frowned. If he hadn't agreed to meet with Denise Bell, he certainly would have been interested in seeing Amanda. He wondered if he'd be able to talk some sense into Denise and get her to go back home to her husband.

He decided to wait for Denise in the hotel dining room and not in his room. She was a stunning and willing woman, and he wasn't all that sure that he'd be able to resist her if he let her in his room.

He informed the desk clerk—the same man Fortune had spoken to about sending a message to Amanda—that he was waiting for someone and would be in the dining room.

58

"The lady we spoke of previously, sir?" the desk clerk asked helpfully.

"No," Clint said, "uh, no, another woman entirely."

"Oh," the clerk said with a knowing look, "I see. I will tell her where you are, sir."

"Thank you."

"Uh, Mr. Adams?"

"Yes?"

The clerk leaned forward, and Clint could smell whatever the man used on his hair to keep it slicked down the way he did.

"If the, uh, other lady in question should arrive and ask for you, shall I tell her that you are still . . . out?"

"That would be a good idea, yes," Clint said. "Thank you for the suggestion."

"Of course, sir," the man said. "We try to serve our guests in every way possible."

"And you do a fine job of it."

The man smiled. Clint went into the dining room and ordered a pot of coffee.

He was surprised at how quickly Denise Bell arrived. She got to the door of the dining room even before his pot of coffee had arrived. Her eyes searched the room, and when she spotted him she smiled and walked to his table.

He stood as she reached him and held a chair for her. She was wearing the same low-cut gown she'd had on earlier, and he wondered where she had told her husband she was going dressed like that.

As she lowered herself into the chair, he found himself looking down her cleavage.

"I was expecting to find you in your room," she said, as he seated himself across from her.

"I thought we'd talk here," he said. "I've ordered some coffee."

"Talking wasn't really what I had in mind, Clint," she said. "I'm sure you know that."

"Yes, I do, Denise," he said. "Nevertheless, I thought we should talk."

She sat back in her chair and allowed her wrap to fall away. Clint could feel the men at the other tables leaning toward them as the creamy flesh of her shoulders came into view.

"All right," she said, "we'll talk . . . for a little while. I really don't have that much time, though. I'll have to get back home fairly soon."

"Where does George think you are?"

She smiled, and oddly enough Clint thought that it was an affectionate smile.

"With a sick friend," she said. "He's so trusting."

"If he's so trusting how can you—" he started and then didn't know how to finish.

"I am wicked, aren't I?" she asked. "Are you going to try and cure me of my wickedness, Clint?"

"Could I do that in one day?"

"One night, maybe," she replied.

At that point the waiter came over with the coffee.

"Shall I pour, sir?" he asked.

"Please."

He poured a cup for Clint.

"For the lady?" The man's eyes were so glued to Denise's breasts that Clint was worried that was where the coffee would go.

"Yes, thank you," Denise said.

"Do you have any pie tonight?" Clint asked.

"Yes, sir. We have some peach pie, and apple."

"I'll have a slice of peach."

"Make mine apple," Denise said.

"I'll bring it right out."

"I thought his eyes were going to fall out of his head," Clint said as the man left. "Does that give you a feeling of power?"

"Of course it does, darling," she said, laughing. "Why else would a woman wear something like this? You were all looking down my dress at dinner, weren't you?"

"I'm looking down your dress now," Clint admitted.

She leaned forward, so that he could have a better view.

"You can see it all if you want to," she said. "All we have to do is go upstairs."

How many men did he know who would have jumped at that suggestion? he wondered. More than wouldn't, that was for sure.

"Why did you marry George, Denise?"

She sat back.

"You really do want to talk, don't you?"

"Yes."

She toyed with her coffee cup for a few moments.

"Will it sound silly if I say I don't know? Yes, of course it does."

"Do you love him?"

"He loves me," she said. "He was one of a few men I was seeing, and he's the one who asked me. I hadn't ever been married before. I suppose the idea just appealed to me." She said the last with a shrug.

"That doesn't sound like a good enough reason to get married."

"Are you married?"

"No."

"Ever been?"

"No."

"Ever been close?"

"Once."

"What happened?"

"She died."

"I'm sorry." She paused, then asked, "You've never even thought about asking anyone else?"

Clint thought briefly of Anne Archer, who usually traveled all over the West with her partners, Sandy Spillane and Katy Littlefeather, collecting bounties.

"No."

"But you've known a lot of women."

"Yes."

"And I'll bet you kept all of them satisfied?"

"I'd like to think so."

Suddenly Clint realized that the direction of the conversation had changed.

"Hey, we're not supposed to be talking about me."

"I know," she said, sitting back, "but I don't like talking about me."

"Why not?"

She made a face.

"I guess I don't like myself very much." She looked at him. "Does it make you happy to hear me say that?"

"No," he said, "no, Denise, it doesn't."

The waiter came with the pie and set it in front of

them, but Denise ignored it. She drew her wrap around her, and Clint knew they were done.

"Well, now that I have admitted it I'll have to be getting back."

"All right."

"Unless you've changed your mind about taking me to your room?"

"I haven't changed my mind," he said. "I'd love to do it, but I won't."

"Well," she said, "it's sweet of you to put it that way."

She stood up, once again attracting the eyes of everyone in the room, men and women.

"I don't suppose I'll see you again before you leave," she said.

"I don't think so."

"Will you do me a favor?"

"What?"

"Will you watch out for George while you're over there? I know it doesn't sound like it, but I do . . . I do care for him."

"I'll keep an eye on him."

"I mean," she said, "I know you're probably supposed to keep Mr. Fortune safe, but if you could spare the time—"

"Don't worry, Denise," he said, "George will come back."

"Good," she said, nodding, "that's good. Good-bye, Clint."

"Good-bye, Denise."

She hesitated a moment, then smiled and returned to the young lady she had been earlier in the evening.

"I'm not going to change my ways, you know," she said. "I can't now."

"I hope you do someday," he said, "before you have to pay for them."

"Oh, I will have to pay for them," she said. "I usually do."

"Well, then, I hope the price isn't too high."

She looked sad for a moment and said, "It usually is," then turned and left the room, taking everyone's eyes to the doorway with her. Then she was gone.

Clint didn't know what good their talk had done, but at least he'd avoided going to his room with her. He cut into his pie, wondering if she was really going home now, or if she was going to find a man who did not have his willpower.

FIFTEEN

Clint finished his pie and Denise's and went to his room. He stopped just short of putting the key in the door and had a thought. What if he had brought Denise up here, and they had entered, only to find Amanda waiting in his bed? What would have been the reaction of the two women?

He put his key in the lock, turned it, and entered. He was immediately aware that someone was in the room. A harsh odor of sweat assailed his nostrils, and he reacted immediately, raising his left arm as someone brought something down on him, aiming for his head. Something hard struck his arm, but he ignored the pain. He drew his gun and fired in one motion. Someone grunted as the bullet struck home, and his assailant staggered back but did not go down. In the light from the hall he saw a man's silhouette, and saw the arm come up again, but not in a striking pose. The man, probably holding a gun, was going to try to fire. Clint beat him to it, firing his gun again. This time the man grunted and went down.

"What the hell—" someone yelled from the hall.

"What's goin' on?" someone else shouted.

Clint ignored them, stepped to the gaslight on the wall, and turned up the flame. He saw the man lying on the floor, a gun next to him. He walked over and kicked the gun away, then bent and checked for a pulse. He found none.

"What's going on?" a man asked from the doorway.

Clint looked up and saw a man with a huge mustache staring down at him, well-dressed and officious-looking. He appeared to be in his mid-forties and looked like more than a curious onlooker.

"Who are you?" Clint asked.

"The house detective."

"You better get the police," Clint said, "and the manager."

"Is he dead?"

"He is."

"Did you—"

"I did," Clint said, standing up and holstering his gun. "He tried to kill me. He was waiting here for me. I'm going to want to know how he got into my room."

"I don't think—"

"Get somebody!" Clint said harshly. "The police, and the manager—now!"

"Mister," the house detective said, "you just relax. I think you better give me your gun before I go for the manager."

"Not likely," Clint said. "This fellow might have a friend around, and as soon as he sees I'm unarmed I'm an easy target."

The house detective, not backing down, nodded and said, "All right, that makes sense. You wait here and I'll go and get the people you want."

"Fine."

"Don't be trying to leave the hotel, though."

"I have no intention of leaving," Clint said. "I've got too many questions that need answering."

"We'll get to 'em," the detective said. "We'll sure get to 'em."

SIXTEEN

The house detective returned with the manager, a man in his sixties, also well-dressed and officious-looking.

"I've sent for the police," the detective told Clint.

"This is terrible," the manager said. "Terrible. This has never happened at the Independence before."

"There's a first time for everything," Clint said. "What's your name, sir?"

The manager looked at him and said, "Faraday, Frederick Faraday."

"And you're the manager?"

"I'm the night manager."

"And your name?" Clint asked the detective.

"Creasey, John Creasey, Mr. Adams."

"You know who I am, huh?"

"I checked the register for your name," Creasey said, "but if you mean do I *know* who you are, the answer is yes."

The manager, Faraday, was looking at both of them in confusion.

"I don't understand."

"Mr. Adams has a reputation in the West," Creasey said, "a reputation it looks like might have followed him here."

"You might be right," Clint said. "This man could be somebody who recognized me, but I'd like to know how he got into my room. I'd also like to know if he's a guest here."

"We'll find all of that out," Creasey said.

"Where is that policeman?" Clint asked.

"I've sent for someone a little more in authority than just a uniformed policeman," Creasey said. "Maybe we should go to my office and wait for him."

Clint looked down at the dead man, then at Creasey.

"All right."

"What about . . . him?" Faraday asked, pointing to the dead man.

"He's not going anywhere, Frederick," Creasey said. "Let's just close the door, and lock it."

"A-all right."

Creasey turned and announced to the people crowding the hall that the show was over and they should all go back into their own rooms.

"Would you like to follow me, Mr. Adams?"

"Lead the way, Mr. Creasey."

•   •   •

Clint found himself liking the house detective, John Creasey. The man did not back down from him at all and also had not taken a stuffy attitude about what had happened.

When they got to his office Creasey asked, "Can I get you some coffee while we're waiting for the police?"

"You can if you can add something to it."

Creasey smiled.

"I've got some brandy that will go well with it."

"Fine."

Shortly they both had a cup of coffee laced with brandy in front of them and were sitting on opposite sides of Creasey's desk. His office was barely large enough to hold the two of them, the desk, and a file cabinet. On the desk was a full pot of coffee and an extra cup.

"Why did you send for someone special?" Clint asked. "Why not just a policeman off the street?"

"The Independence Hotel has a reputation to protect, Mr. Adams," Creasey said. "What happened is tragic, and needs to be explained, but it also needs to be contained. You can understand my position."

"Yes, as a matter of fact, I can," Clint said, "and I'm sure you can understand mine."

"You're upset that someone was in your room, and that you were shot at," Creasey said. "You, uh, aren't injured are you?"

"Actually, my left arm is kind of sore. He tried to hit me with his gun before he tried to shoot me with it."

"We have a doctor on call, if you think—"

"No, no," Clint said, "I've been hit before. I'm fine."

"I'm also sure you've been shot at before."

"Many times," Clint said. "but it's never a pleasurable experience."

"No," Creasey said, "it's not," speaking like a man who had been through it himself.

Before Clint could ask about that there was a knock at the door. Instead of simply calling out for whoever it was to come in, Creasey stood up and opened the door himself.

"Ah, Danny," Creasey said, "thanks for coming."

The man who walked in looked disheveled, did not have any of the look that Creasey and Faraday had presented. In fact, he looked like a man who had just gotten out of bed and dressed hurriedly. He was roughly the same age as Clint and Creasey. He didn't look happy.

"Johnny," the man said, "this better be good. Is that coffee I smell?"

"Sit down and have a cup," Creasey said, closing the door behind the man, "but first meet one of our guests. This is Clint Adams. Mr. Adams, this is Lieutenant Dan O'Shay of the Philadelphia Police Department."

"How do," O'Shay said. "That coffee?"

"Coming up," Creasey said. He poured a cup, added brandy, and handed it to the lieutenant.

"No Irish whiskey?" the man asked.

"Brandy."

He sighed, as if heavily put-upon.

"I suppose it will have to do. Now, why don't you tell me why you brought me here."

"Have a seat, Dan," Creasey said, "and I'll explain."

SEVENTEEN

Lieutenant O'Shay listened to what John Creasey had to say without interruption. Once he leaned forward and added brandy to his cup without adding more coffee. When the house detective was finished, the policeman put his cup on the desk and turned to Clint.

"Did you know the man?"

"No."

"Have you ever seen him before?"

"No."

"What are you doing in Philadelphia?"

"I came to see a friend."

"Who?"

"Sam Fortune."

O'Shay's bushy eyebrows rose.

"You have interesting friends."

"Yes, I do."

"How long are you intending to stay in Philadelphia?" O'Shay asked.

"A day or two longer, no more."

"Do you intend to kill anyone else?"

"Only if they try to kill me first."

O'Shay looked at Creasey and said, "That sounds fair enough."

Creasey nodded.

"Do you know the dead man?" O'Shay asked Creasey.

"Yes."

Clint looked at Creasey, surprised.

"You didn't tell me that."

Creasey looked at him.

"I wasn't sure about you."

"And you are now?"

Creasey smiled.

"No."

"Who's the dead man?" O'Shay asked Creasey.

"Arnold Fenton."

"Arnie Fenton?" O'Shay was surprised now.

"Who's Fenton?" Clint asked.

"Well," O'Shay said, "if we were out west where you come from, Adams, we'd call him a hired gun."

"And what do you call him here in the East?"

O'Shay looked at Clint.

"A hired gun."

"Whose hired gun is he?"

"Arnie would work for anyone who had the money," O'Shay said.

"Not anymore," Creasey said.

"No," O'Shay agreed, "not anymore."

"What do you want to do about this, Dan?" Creasey asked.

O'Shay looked at Creasey, then at Clint, and then back to the house detective.

"Are you satisfied that Mr. Adams here is telling the truth?"

"Yes," Creasey said without hesitation.

"Are you prepared to continue to let him stay here?"

"I'd have to check with the management," Creasey said, "but that would be my recommendation."

O'Shay looked at Clint again.

"One or two days?"

"At most."

"Well," O'Shay said, scratching his head and then his beard stubble, "I don't see any reason to try to make you leave before that."

"I appreciate that," Clint said dryly.

"Sam Fortune, huh?" O'Shay said. "Interesting friends."

Clint didn't say anything.

"Have you and Mr. Fortune known each other a long time?"

"Not a very long time," Clint said. "A few years."

"Do you work for him, or are you just friends?"

"We're friends."

"That's interesting," O'Shay said.

"Why?"

"I didn't know he had any friends. Do you think this fella trying to kill you has anything to do with your friendship with Fortune?"

"I don't know. You tell me. Does he usually work in that circle?"

"Like I said," O'Shay answered, "Arnie would work for anybody who had the money to hire him. People like Sam Fortune . . ." The policeman let his sentence trail off without finishing.

Clint decided not to pursue the matter and let it lie.

"Well," O'Shay said, standing up, "I might as well take a look at the body, and have it removed. Johnny, I think you'll have to give Mr. Adams here a new room."

"That won't be a problem."

"Let's get this done, then, so I can get back to sleep. I know my wife will be waiting up. She always does when I'm called out of the house late."

"How is Annie?" Creasey asked, also rising.

"Cranky," O'Shay said. "She always is when I'm called out of the house late."

Clint rose and looked at the two men who were obviously good friends.

"If you'd like to wait here," Creasey said, "I'll get you a new room. You can move your belongings into it in the morning."

"That'll be fine."

"Mr. Adams," O'Shay said, "it's been interesting. I hope I won't have to see you again before you leave town."

"Believe me, Lieutenant," Clint said, "I hope so, too."

EIGHTEEN

The next morning Baker Jack stood in front of his boss's desk.

"It's all over the newspapers," the man said. "It was a goddamned stupid move."

"It wasn't me."

"This is not what I had in mind, Jack."

"It wasn't me."

"I expected more from yo—what'd you say?"

For the third time he repeated, "It wasn't me. I didn't have anything to do with it."

"Well, then . . . who did?"

"I don't know."

"Arnie Fenton did some work with you, didn't he?"

"He did."

"Do you have any idea who else he worked for?"

Jack spread his hands.

"Anybody who'd pay him."

"So who'd pay him to do this?"

"To tell you the truth," Jack said, "I thought you did."

"Me? Why would I hire him? I've got you."

"There's another possibility."

"Like what?"

"Like maybe Arnie just recognized the Gunsmith and thought he'd make a name for himself."

The other man thought that over.

"Yeah, I guess that is a possibility, isn't it?" he finally said.

Baker Jack didn't respond.

"Well," his boss finally said, "whatever his reason was, Arnie hasn't done us any favors. From now on Adams and Fortune are going to be on their guard."

"I think they were anyway," Jack said. "Arnie was pretty good, and I hear Adams took care of him with no problem."

"Was Arnie as good as you?"

Baker didn't think the question was worth answering, but he said, "No."

"So then you won't have this problem, will you?"

"No."

"Nevertheless," his boss said, "I think we're going to have to wait until we get over there."

"Where?"

"Paris."

"You want me to go to Paris?"

"That was always a possibility."

"I thought we'd take care of it here."

"Yes, well, I thought so, too, but now we're not,"

the other man said. "I understand Dan O'Shay was called in on this last night."

"So?"

"So I don't want to have anything to do with him. We'll do this in Europe. I'll see about getting us tickets."

"On a boat?"

"Yes, on a boat. How else do you think we'd get there?"

"A boat," Baker Jack said with distaste.

"Don't tell me you've never been on a boat?"

"Never."

"Well, you'll like it."

"I doubt it."

"They've got food, and women, and gambling. You'll love it."

"I like all of that," Jack said, "but not on a boat."

"And think about bringing two more men," the other man said, "just to be on the safe side."

"Two more? I can do this myself—"

"Just do it, Baker," the man said. "It will make me feel better to have reinforcements along, just in case we need them."

Baker Jack sighed.

"All right. I know just who to get."

"Fine," the man said. "Now get out of here and let me get to work. Go get yourself some breakfast."

"Should I come back this evening? Let you know about the other two men?"

"I trust your judgment. I'll meet them the day we set sail."

"On a boat," Baker Jack said again with disgust.

"Yes," the other man said, "on a boat."

NINETEEN

The next day Clint went out to do some shopping for himself. George Bell had bought him the clothes he'd need for this trip, but there were bound to be other items that only he could buy for himself.

Halfway through the day he still hadn't bought anything. He found himself in the section of Philadelphia where he knew Sam Fortune had his office. Had he come here on purpose, or simply drifted here by coincidence? Since he rarely, if ever, believed in coincidence, he decided that his subconscious had brought him here for a reason, and that reason was to talk to Fortune about what had happened last night.

Clint presented himself at Fortune's office to his secretary, a rigid-backed woman whose name, he recalled, was Miss Simpson. She had a severe mouth and an almost as severe bun on top of her head.

"I'll see if Mr. Fortune has time to see you," she said.

"Thank you, Miss Simpson."

She disappeared into her master's office, and reappeared moments later. Clint could hear Fortune's voice booming out at her, "—keep my friend waiting any longer, damn you!"

There was no sign on Miss Simpson's face that indicated Fortune had been berating her.

"You may go in."

"Thank you."

Clint entered the office, closing the door behind him.

"Damn that woman for making you wait," Fortune shouted from his seated position behind his desk. There was a huge window behind him that offered an incredible view of the city.

"She was just doing her job."

"Well," Fortune said, "your defense of her has saved her job. I won't fire her. Come, come, sit down. I'll get you some brandy. Maybe I'll have some, too."

Since there was already a glass on his desk Clint surmised that his friend had already had some and was simply going to have more.

Fortune went to the side bar as Clint sat down. He refilled his own glass and filled one for Clint.

"Here," he said, handing it to Clint and then sitting back behind his desk. "To a successful trip."

"I'll drink to that," Clint said, taking a sip, then adding, "especially after what happened last night." .

"What happened last night, then?" Fortune asked.

"Somebody tried to kill me in my room."

Fortune choked on his brandy, wiped his mouth, and blurted, "What?"

"He was waiting in my room when I got back from—when I got back."

"What happened?"

"I had to kill him."

"Who was he?"

"The house detective said his name was Arnold Fenton."

Fortune shook his head.

"I didn't know him. Did the police respond?"

"The house detective, a man named Creasey, called for a friend of his, Lieutenant O'Shay."

"Dan O'Shay."

"You know him, then?"

"I've met him once or twice," Fortune said. "He has political aspirations. It figures he'd be called in to, uh, protect the reputation of the Independence Hotel. He didn't give you a hard time, did he?"

"No, not at all," Clint said.

"And the hotel?"

"They gave me a new room."

"I know Creasey, as well."

That surprised Clint.

"How?"

"He used to be like O'Shay," Fortune said.

"How do you mean?"

"He used to be a policeman with political aspirations."

"And what happened?"

"There was some, uh, difficulty; he had to leave his position with the police department."

"What happened then?"

"He was hired immediately by the Independence to be their house detective. Actually, he calls himself a house detective. They refer to him as their Director of Security."

"And how long has he been doing that?"

"About three years now, I think. During that time his friend O'Shay was promoted to lieutenant, and I believe he is not far from becoming a captain."

"You seem to know a lot about them."

Fortune smiled.

"I know a lot about a lot of people," he said, waggling his eyebrows up and down. "Well, I guess somebody knows that you're going with me to Paris."

"Maybe," Clint said.

"What other explanation could there be?"

"He might have recognized me."

"Here? In Philadelphia? Oh, yes, I guess you're right. You do have a reputation, don't you? You know, sometimes I forget about that."

"I don't. Sam, tell me who you think might try to kill me, or you, to keep you from going on the Orient Express."

Fortune frowned.

"If I could narrow it down to three, or four, or half a dozen, I'd tell you and you could check them out, but I can't, and we don't have time anyway. We're leaving tomorrow."

"Tomorrow?"

"Early," Fortune said. "Eight a.m."

Clint didn't tell him that eight a.m. was not considered

"early" by people who lived in the West and were up at first light.

"Have you told George?"

"Of course," Fortune said. "He went to get the tickets. Did, uh, anything else happen last night?"

"Like what?"

"Oh, I thought maybe Mrs. Bell might have paid you a visit."

"I'm afraid not."

"Then you were alone when you were attacked?"

"Yes," Clint said, "I was alone."

"What about Amanda?"

"Alone is alone, Sam."

"Okay, okay," Fortune said. "Look, why don't you come to my house tonight and stay there. We can look out for each other, huh?"

"I think that might be a good idea," Clint said, although he was thinking only of looking out for Fortune, and not vice versa. "I'll go to the hotel now, check out, and come by your house."

"I'll be there by the time you get there," Fortune said. He gave Clint the address and told him any carriage driver would be able to take him there.

"You weren't injured last night, were you?"

"No," Clint said, standing. He set his empty glass down on Fortune's desk. "I'll see you in about an hour, then."

"An hour."

Clint left, drawing not even a look from the severe Miss Simpson, whose job he had saved.

TWENTY

Sam Fortune had a three-story house in a very wealthy section of the city. He held the door open while Clint was paying the driver.

"What took you so long?"

"I guess I found the one driver in town who couldn't find you easily."

He entered the house carrying his one bag and his rifle. Fortune closed the door behind him. A man wearing black pants and a white jacket stood just inside, waiting. He appeared to be over sixty and stood barely five foot four.

"Cyril will take you up to your room on the second floor," Fortune said. "Just don't expect him to carry anything, not at his age."

In response to that Cyril reached out and took Clint's bag.

"Follow me, sir."

Clint looked at Fortune, who said, "The old goat knows I love him. Go on, get settled in your room and then come down for a drink before dinner."

"All right," Clint said, starting up the steps after Cyril.

"And when you come back down," Fortune called after him, "I'll have a surprise for you."

The room was twice as large as his room at the hotel had been, and much more plush. He'd been in the homes of wealthy people before, but never anyone as rich as Sam Fortune. He couldn't imagine what it felt like to have so much money.

"Dinner in half an hour, sir," Cyril said, depositing his bag on the huge bed. "Mr. Fortune will be waiting for you in the den."

"All right, Cyril. Thank you."

The man backed out of the room and closed the door.

Clint prowled the room for a few moments, then decided to go downstairs for that drink.

He found the den after two false starts into other rooms.

"There you are," Fortune said.

"This is an easy house to get lost in."

"I know," Fortune said, carrying a brandy across the room to Clint. There were plush chairs strategically placed around a sofa, and in one corner an ornate writing table or desk. "It's too big, I know, but you know I always expected to get married someday."

"You did?"

"Well . . . someday, maybe." A melancholy look came over Fortune's face, one that Clint had never seen before. "I once thought I might fill this house with children."

"You still could."

Fortune smiled.

"What decent woman would have me, Clint?"

"Why marry a decent one, then?"

Fortune stared at Clint, then raised an eyebrow.

"Why, indeed?"

There was a knock at the door then and Fortune's face brightened and broadened into a smile.

"There's my surprise. Cyril will let them in."

"Who?"

"You'll see."

It took a few moments, and then Cyril appeared at the door.

"Your guests have arrived, sir."

"Show them in, Cyril."

The man disappeared, then reappeared and ushered two women into the room. Clint recognized both. One was Dolly, the blonde who had been with Fortune the evening before.

The other was Amanda.

TWENTY-ONE

They sat down to dinner, Clint and Fortune at opposite ends of the long table, Dolly to Fortune's right, Amanda to Clint's right.

"I understand you're leaving tomorrow," Amanda said when they were seated and served.

"Yes," Clint said, "I was just informed today that we'd be leaving at eight a.m."

"I . . . appreciated your message last night," she said. "It saved me a trip to the hotel."

"Another surprise that Sam sprung on me at the last minute," Clint said. "I'm sorry."

"That's all right," she said, putting her hand over his on the table. "I'm here now."

"What are you two talking about?" Fortune demanded from his end of the table, which was far enough away that he could not hear their conversation.

"Surprises," Clint said.

"Ah," Fortune said, smiling and looking at Dolly. He picked up his wineglass. "Here's to surprises," he toasted.

"Surprises," they all said.

Later, when Clint and Amanda had worn themselves out and were lying together on the huge bed, she said, "You'll have to come back to Philadelphia, won't you? I mean, when you return on the ship?"

"Unless I stop off in New York," he said.

"And why would you do that?"

"I have friends in New York."

"Female friends?"

"Some."

She lay silent for a while, with her head on his chest, then said, "I've never been to New York."

"It's not so different from Philadelphia," he said. "Only bigger."

"I wonder what Paris will be like."

"I don't know. I've never been there."

"Neither have I."

More silence.

"I'm not hinting, you know?"

"Huh?"

"I mean, about going to New York or Paris with you. I'm not hinting."

"I know that."

"I'm just . . . talking."

"Mmmm."

"I'd like you to come back here, you know."

"I'd like to come back."

"Then you will?"

"Depends."

"On what?"

"On what happens in Paris," he said, "and Istanbul."

And points in between, he added silently. Also what happened on the ship. Where would they make another try? he wondered. On the ship, or after they docked in New York, or Paris?

"Hmm?" he said, aware that she'd continued speaking.

"I said even if you come back for a few days or so, I doubt we'd see each other again after that."

"Mmmm."

"So I'll take what I can get."

"That's all we can do," he said.

"In fact," she said, rolling onto him, "I'll take what I can get now."

She slipped her hand between them and started to rub him, then pull on him, until he was hard. That done she lifted her hips and came down on him. She was excited, and wet, and he slid right in with a groan.

"Yes!" she said, sitting up on him and riding him up and down.

He soon forgot about the ship, New York, Europe, and everything else except for the girl on top of him.

TWENTY-TWO

"New York," George Bell said.

"Yep." Clint was standing beside him, both of them looking at New York from the ship that would take them to Paris.

"Have you been there?" Bell asked.

"Yes," Clint said, "many times."

"I wish we were getting off here, at least for a while," Bell said. "I've never been there."

"Maybe on the return trip," Clint said.

Bell turned his back on New York and looked at Clint with a grave expression.

"Do you think we'll be coming back?"

"Why shouldn't we?"

"Well . . . if someone is out to kill you, or Mr. Fortune, or . . ."—he swallowed hard—"me."

"Nobody's out to kill you, George."

"Yes, but I'm along for the ride," Bell said. "I could get killed, couldn't I?"

"If you feel that way," Clint said, "then get off here. I can get Sam to give you enough money to get back to Philadelphia, maybe even stay a few days in New York first."

"He'd fire me."

"No," Clint said, "I won't let him."

"I'd quit, then."

"Why?"

"Because if I can't do my job I shouldn't be working for him."

Clint saw that they were getting ready to pull in the gangplank.

"Well, make up your mind, George," Clint said. "In or out?"

"In," Bell said quickly. "I'm in."

"Then say good-bye to New York."

Bell turned and looked at the great city again.

"Come on," Clint said, "let's find our cabins."

During the ride from Fortune's house to the dock on the morning they left they had gone over all the arrangements.

"We'll each have our own cabin," Fortune said.

"Me, too?" Bell asked in surprise.

"Yes, George, you, too. You made the arrangements for three cabins, didn't you?"

"Uh, yes, sir."

"Did you think I was bringing someone else along?"

"I, uh, didn't know, sir. I mean, you are very popular with the ladies—"

"There will be plenty of ladies on board, George."

"Yes, sir."

"For all of us."

"Oh," Bell said uncomfortably, "I don't think that I would—I mean, I won't be—uh—"

"I hope my cabin is near yours, Sam," Clint said, taking the young man off the hook.

"We'll have three abreast," Fortune said.

"Then you can have the middle one," Clint said, "and George and I will flank you."

"Fine."

They had to take one ship from Philadelphia to New York, and then change. This one was much larger, but they still had three cabins across.

"Here you are, sir," the steward who led them to their cabins said. "I believe Mr. Fortune is already inside."

"Thank you."

As the man left, Clint said to George, "I want to check on Sam. Come with me."

They walked to the door of Fortune's cabin and knocked.

"Come!" Fortune's voice called.

They entered and found Fortune seated in a big easy chair.

"Don't get excited," he said. "All of them don't have this chair. I arranged for it."

"I hope you and your chair are very comfortable," Clint said.

"Are you boys settled in?"

"Not yet," Clint said, "I wanted to check on you first."

"I'm fine."

"Uh, Sam, you do have a gun, don't you?"

"Now, what would I do with a gun, Clint?" Fortune asked. "You know I can't hit anything."

Clint turned to George Bell.

"Do you have one?"

"No," Bell said. "I can't hit anything either."

"Great," Clint said. "Once we're out to sea we'll have to have some lessons."

"We'll be firing guns on board?" Bell asked, surprised.

"I'm sure Sam can arrange anything," Clint said. "We'll just fire out over the water, where the bullets can't do any harm."

"We can put some targets in the water," Fortune said. "It'll be fun."

"Yeah," Clint said, "fun."

"When do they serve dinner on this tub?" Fortune asked. "I'm starving."

"I think the steward said they'd be serving in an hour in the main dining room."

"Great," Fortune said. "And after that we can go gambling."

"I, uh—"

"What is it, George?" Fortune asked. "Don't tell me you've never gambled."

"Uh, no, I haven't."

Fortune looked at Clint and said, "We'll have to have some lessons in that, too."

"At least it'll give us something to do on the trip," Clint said.

TWENTY-THREE

Clint was not surprised to find that he, Bell, and Fortune were seated at the captain's table for dinner. Such was Sam Fortune's stature that this happened without his hand being involved. Apparently, the captain kept track of who his passengers were, and he sent a message down to Fortune's cabin inviting him and his "staff" to dine with him and his other guests.

"Do we know who these other guests are?" Clint asked as they walked to the main dining room.

"Nope," Fortune said. "It'll be interesting to see, though."

"Maybe one of your competitors?"

Fortune laughed.

"If one of them is on board they'll be staying out of my sight. I'm the only American with an invite to this Orient Express gala."

"If one of them is on board," Clint said, "maybe that'll tip us off to who was behind the attack on me."

"You convinced now that it had something to do with all of this?"

"I am," Clint said. "I just don't buy it as a coincidence."

"You don't buy anything as a coincidence," Fortune said.

"Exactly."

When they reached the dining room they were immediately intercepted by a steward who showed them to the captain's table.

"Mr. Fortune?" the captain asked, rising and extending his hand.

"That's right." Fortune accepted the proffered handshake.

"Sir, I am Captain Slaughter, your humble servant on this trip. It's a great pleasure to meet you."

"Thank you, Captain," Fortune said. "These are my associates, Mr. George Bell and Mr. Clint Adams."

"Clint Adams?" a voice asked.

They looked at the people already seated at the captain's table. There were three men and two women, and the voice they had heard was a woman's.

"That's right," Clint said, looking at both women. Each was attractive in her own way. One was fortyish, very appealing in a matronly way, with a firm bosom and a luscious, lascivious mouth.

The other was younger by fifteen years or so, probably all of twenty-five, with bright blue eyes, a firm jaw, and slender shoulders.

"*The* Clint Adams?" the younger woman asked.

"What do you mean, *the* Clint Adams?" the other woman asked.

"Well," the younger woman said, "the Clint Adams I've heard of—"

"I'm the only Clint Adams I know of," Clint said, interrupting her. "And you are?"

"Allow me to introduce the other members of our party," the captain said, "as you take your seats."

There were only three seats available, abreast, starting with the one to the captain's immediate left, extending to the one next to the matronly woman.

Fortune took the first seat, Bell the second, and Clint found himself sitting next to one woman and directly across from the other one.

"Mr. Adams, the lovely lady to your left is Mrs. Gloria Aldred, and next to her is her husband, Mr. Kirby Aldred."

Clint had not heard of either but said hello. Aldred nodded, not bothering to reach across his wife for a handshake. In fact, he started to but was frozen by her look. Instead, Gloria Aldred shook his hand and held it a moment or two too long.

"A pleasure," she said, leaning close to him as she said it. Her perfume was heady, as was the woman herself.

"Across from Mr. Adams is Miss Heather McKay. Miss McKay is a newspaperwoman on her way to Paris to cover the inaugural run of the Orient Express from Paris to Istanbul."

"How exciting for you," Gloria Aldred said.

"Thank you."

"To Miss McKay's left is Mr. Christian James, and here on my right is Mr. Adam De Noux."

"Gentlemen," Clint said. Bell and Fortune inclined their heads in greeting to everyone.

It became very apparent during dinner that the captain knew who Sam Fortune was, and was a big fan. He had a lengthy conversation with Fortune about railroads and shipping and where there was more money to be had, and virtually ignored his other guests, who were left to converse among themselves.

"So, tell us, Miss McKay," Gloria Aldred said, "what is it that is so special about Mr. Adams?"

"You don't recognize the name?" Heather McKay asked in surprise.

"I'm afraid my wife doesn't read very much of what's in the newspapers, my dear, except for the society page."

"Are there other pages?" his wife asked, and they both laughed.

"Well," Heather said, "he's very famous in the West, but I think I'll leave it to him to tell you about it, if he likes."

Clint thanked Heather McKay with his eyes. Yes, she'd brought the whole subject up, but she had apparently decided not to pursue it, maybe because she didn't like the Aldreds very much.

"What about it, Mr. Adams?" Gloria asked. "Will you tell us of your fame?"

"I'm afraid Miss McKay and other newspaper writers over the years have exaggerated my, uh, fame, Mrs. Aldred. I'd actually rather not discuss it, and concentrate more on enjoying this trip."

"Well," Gloria Aldred said, sniffing her disapproval, "if you don't want to talk about it . . ." And she turned her attention elsewhere.

George Bell leaned over and said to Clint, "I could fill them in later, if you like."

"On what?"

"On your, er, fame."

"What do you know about it?"

"I did some research."

"Don't believe everything you read, George."

"But if only half of it is true—"

"Never mind," Clint said. "I don't like my life to be talked about for the entertainment of people like the Aldreds."

"You don't like to talk about yourself much, do you?" Bell asked.

"No," Clint said. "I'd rather enjoy the present than talk about the past. Speaking of the present, here comes dinner. I'm starved. I hope the food is decent on this boat."

TWENTY-FOUR

Later, when Fortune took Bell with him to the gambling deck, Clint decided to go to the bar. As much as he liked to gamble, he didn't feel like it tonight. He felt that Fortune, among all of the gamblers on the boat, would be safe enough. The attack on Clint showed him that these people—whoever they were—seemed to prefer to attack in private.

He was standing at the bar, nursing a beer, when he saw Heather McKay walk in. She was pretty enough, but his instinct was to stay away from her. Unfortunately, before he could act she spotted him and came over.

"Buy a lady a drink?" she asked.

"Of course."

She was taller than she had looked while seated, long and slender, very attractive, and young enough to still give off an air of energy—an air which, for instance, had been totally lacking in Gloria Aldred.

"What will you have?"

"A beer will be fine," she said. "To tell the truth, I'm not much of a wine drinker. I think it comes from being around newspaper reporters all the time—the men, I mean. All they do is smoke and drink beer."

"Do you smoke?"

She shook her head. "I never developed a taste for it."

Clint signaled the bartender to bring two beers.

"I'm sorry about what happened at dinner," she said. "When I heard your name I just blurted it out."

"That's all right," he said. "In my eyes you redeemed yourself."

She made a face. "I just didn't like that woman, or her husband. He came after me as soon as we got on board."

"Can't much blame him for that," he said.

"I'll take that as a compliment, coming from you," she said. "He, on the other hand, is just an old lech."

The beers arrived and Clint handed her one of them, recalling that Kirby Aldred had not seemed to be much older than he was.

"There's a table," Clint said, gesturing with his free hand. "Would you like to sit?"

"Yes, thank you."

They walked to the free table, one of about half in the room that were actually empty. Clint assumed that the people who were not still at dinner were probably gambling.

"Did I understand that you were going to Paris to cover the Orient Express?" he asked.

"Yes," she said. "I managed to convince my editor that it was an important story."

"And got yourself a trip to Europe in the process."

"That, too," she said, "but do you know how I convinced him?"

"No," he said, "impress me."

"I heard that Sam Fortune was going," she said. "I told him that where Fortune went there was a story in the making."

"I suppose that's true enough."

"I also heard—and maybe you can tell me if this is true—that there were people who didn't want Mr. Fortune to make the trip."

"I don't know that I—"

"Wait a minute!" she said, her eyes lighting up. She sat back and stared at Clint, as if she had just discovered something wonderful on his face—but he didn't think that was the case.

"That's why you're here," she said. "To make sure he gets there. You're along to keep him alive."

Clint sipped his beer and watched her over the rim of the mug.

"Did he hire you?"

"I don't hire out my gun, Miss McKay," he said. "Besides, Sam and I are friends."

"So then he just asked you to come along?"

"He invited me," he said. "He thought I'd find it interesting, and I have never been to Paris or to Istanbul."

"So then you are along to keep him alive?"

"I think," Clint said, "that if anyone tried to harm him, I would certainly do my best to stop them."

She leaned over to examine him and said, "I don't see you wearing a gun."

"They frown on guns out in the open on cruise ships, Miss McKay."

"Aha," she said, "then you do have one on you, I just can't see it."

As a matter of fact he had his little Colt New Line tucked into his belt at the small of his back, but he didn't tell her that.

"This is a great story."

"There's no story that I can see," he said. "At least, not regarding me."

"Well . . . I can say that you were on this ship without getting sued by you, can't I?"

"Why would I sue you for saying that?"

"I can telegraph the story back to my paper," she said. "Sam Fortune and the Gunsmith."

He made a face, but he certainly couldn't stop her from referring to him that way either.

"Write what you want, Miss McKay," he said, "just be careful of the conclusions you draw."

"Oh, don't worry," she said, pushing her half finished mug of beer away and standing up, "I'm always very careful what I write. See you later, Mr. Adams."

"Clint," he said. "If you're going to write about me, you might as well call me Clint."

"Clint," she said, "thank you for talking to me. I'm Heather, by the way, not Miss McKay. Maybe I'll see you in the casino?"

"Maybe you will, yes," he said. She smiled and hurried away.

TWENTY-FIVE

Clint wondered what Heather McKay would actually write, since she knew he wouldn't have a chance to see it until they got back to the United States, and then maybe not at all. She seemed straightforward enough, but he had learned a long time ago that newspaper writers were a breed apart. They'd do anything for a story—anything.

He drank his beer and took his time doing it. He enjoyed watching the other passengers around him, and played a game with himself, making up stories about them, since they were all total strangers.

Almost.

''What the hell—'' he said as his eyes fell on a man sitting with a stunning red-haired woman. Actually, he'd been looking at the woman admiringly and had only glanced at her male companion. Now that he took a better look he realized he knew the man.

Well, "knew" was a strong word. He had probably spoken with him three times in their lives, but all three times it had been across a poker table. His name was Oliver Carew, and he hated his name and so he insisted that everyone call him "Chance." When Clint first met him, someone—it might have been Luke Short—said that Chance Carew was also known as "Check-and-Raise" Carew because he was particularly notorious for using that strategy during a poker game.

What, he wondered, was Carew doing on this boat? Certainly the redheaded woman was reason enough. She was tall; he knew that even though she was seated because he could see her legs, which seemed incredibly long. She was wearing a green gown, which he knew would match her eyes. The gown was off the shoulder on one side, revealing a freckled shoulder, and although he could not see her breasts at the moment, he knew they would be freckled, as well. What was it about red-haired women, he wondered, that made it so easy for them to get away with having freckles?

Clint considered walking over and asking Carew what he was doing on the boat, but he decided to wait until the man was alone. He'd probably run across him in the casino, anyway, since there was little chance that a man like Carew would not appear there.

Clint finished his beer and decided to go on up to the casino himself to have a look around. There would be time enough for talking when Carew put in his appearance.

•   •   •

Baker Jack knew that he and his boss had taken a chance by traveling on the same ship with Sam Fortune and his people. His boss understood the risk, too, which was why he was taking all of his meals in his cabin. He was taking no chances that Fortune would spot him.

On the other hand, Fortune did not know Baker Jack on sight, nor did he know the two men who Jack had chosen to accompany him and his boss on the trip.

Jack had dispatched the two men to the casino after dinner, to keep an eye on Fortune and his man. Baker Jack chose to keep an eye on Clint Adams himself. He followed him from dinner to the bar, and ultimately to the casino. Jack was now standing just inside the casino, watching Clint Adams, who, at the moment, was doing nothing but standing very still.

He appeared to be listening.

When Clint reached the casino deck of the ship he knew where all the people had gone after dinner. When he'd left the bar it had still been no more than half full. This deck, however, was teeming with people, and with noise—special noise. Standing just inside the door, he could hear the ball bouncing on a roulette wheel, and he could hear a dealer at a table somewhere flipping the cards over audibly. He could hear the sound of chips falling, or simply being played with by their owner while he tried to decide whether to raise, call, or fold.

They were sounds that were comforting to him, because he knew what they meant, and what they promised, and what they threatened. They were the very distinctive sounds of gambling.

He decided to simply take a turn around the casino

and see what it had to offer. Perhaps, during that time, he would run into Fortune and Bell.

"Mr. Adams."

Clint turned at the sound of a woman's voice and saw Gloria Aldred approaching him. There was no denying her appeal. She was full-bodied and handsome, and in her youth had probably been no less than beautiful. He did not, however, like her in the least since their dinner together, and did not have a thing to say to her.

"My husband has abandoned me," she said.

"Has he?"

"Yes, he has," she said, "in favor of one game of chance or another."

Abruptly she took hold of his arm.

"Perhaps you would like to keep me company?"

"Mrs. Aldred—"

"Gloria."

"Gloria, I don't think—"

"I don't mean here," she said, her voice suddenly throaty, "I mean in cabin four-eleven."

"Cabin . . . your cabin?"

"Yes, dear man, my cabin."

She breathed deeply, and her impressive cleavage swelled. He was sure this was something she rehearsed, because she did it so well.

"Isn't that the cabin you share with your husband?" he asked.

"Yes, but he'll be here for hours and hours," she said. "There is absolutely no danger."

"Really."

"Yes," she said, releasing his arm. "I'm going there

now. Why don't you give me a half an hour to freshen up?"

"Half an hour?"

"Yes."

"All right, Gloria," he said suddenly, "a half an hour it is."

"Wonderful." Her eyes seemed to glow from within, and he knew she was sexually aroused. "I will see you in half an hour, then."

"Wild horses couldn't keep me away," he said in a low tone.

"Perhaps," she said, matching his tone, "you will even show me why you seem so . . . dangerous."

"I just might be able to do that."

She smiled and left. He watched as she walked to the main entrance of the casino. A man standing just inside the door was watching her as she approached, stepped aside to allow her to pass, and then watched as she left.

Under other circumstances Clint would have been at her door in twenty-nine minutes. However, even if she hadn't been married, he didn't like her, and certainly had no intention of going to her cabin for any reason.

There were, after all, plenty of other women on board.

TWENTY-SIX

Clint found Bell watching Sam Fortune play high-stakes blackjack. Clint didn't like blackjack. The return of two-and-a-half to one on blackjack didn't appeal to him—but when you played for the stakes Sam Fortune played, it made a difference.

"How's he doing?" Clint asked.

Bell started and turned to look at Clint.

"Jesus," he said, "don't sneak up on me like that. He's losing a fortune. I don't understand how he can keep betting as much as he is."

"He's waiting for the cards to change."

"How can the cards change?" Bell asked.

"Actually, I'm talking about his luck, George," Clint said. "Sam believes that you have to keep banging away at the house until the cards start to come your way."

"What house?" Bell asked, confused.

"Did Sam explain the game to you at all?"

"No," Bell said, "he just said I should watch and learn, but I need someone to explain it to me."

"Come on," Clint said, "let's find a smaller stakes table and I'll show you how to play the game."

Clint and Bell found an empty blackjack table where the dealer was looking bored. As they approached Clint realized that it was empty because the stakes were low.

"Here we go," he said to Bell. "Sit down."

"Me?"

"You."

"I—I don't know the first thing about gambling," Bell protested.

"We're going to fix that right now, George," Clint said, and sat next to him.

Over the course of the next hour Clint explained first the fundamentals of blackjack, then began to explain strategies. During that time George Bell managed to win fifty dollars.

"You seem to have the other ingredient that's important in this game," said Clint, who was losing a hundred.

"What's that?"

"Luck," Clint said.

"You mean luck figures into this?"

"It figures into it a whole lot," Clint said. "I've seen men who know every strategy there is to know who can never win because they have bad luck."

"And my luck is good?"

"You're ahead, aren't you?"

"Yes," Bell said. "I can't believe it. Fifty dollars!"

"So far," Clint said.

"So far? You mean, I can't keep this money?"

The dealer watched and listened to the conversation with interest.

"You could keep it, George, but the point of having good luck is to ride it."

"How do you ride luck?"

"What I mean is, you have to push your luck, take it as far as it will go. Okay, here, I'll show you. Bet the fifty dollars."

"What?" They had been betting five dollars at a time, and Bell seemed horrified at the prospect of betting fifty dollars—his entire profit—at one time. "I can't."

"You can," Clint said. "Just do it."

"Clint—"

"You're going to win, George."

"How do you know?"

"Because you're lucky."

Slowly, reluctantly, feeling sick to his stomach, George Bell pushed fifty dollars worth of chips—his entire profit!—forward.

"Betting fifty dollars," the dealer said. "Dealing."

And he dealt George Bell two cards, one facing down, the other facing up.

TWENTY-SEVEN

"I can't believe it," George Bell said.

They were sitting in a small bar at the back of the casino, where winners could celebrate with a drink and losers could commiserate with several drinks.

"I can't believe it," Bell said again.

"Believe it, kid," Clint said. "Here, have a drink."

Bell took the beer that Clint pushed across the table to him and drank half of it.

"Is this what it's supposed to feel like?" Bell asked.

"Well," Clint said, "I sort of feel like you're over-reacting a little."

"Here you fellas are," Sam Fortune said, appearing at their table. "Don't go away, I'm gonna get a beer."

Fortune went to the bar. Clint stared across the table at George Bell, who seemed to be in another world. His eyes were glazed, and he was staring at nothing in particular.

Fortune returned and sat between them.

"I'm coming back," he said eagerly. "Just taking a break. I was losing a bundle, but I've cut my losses in half. I'm gonna take 'em later tonight." He took a swallow of his beer. "What have you fellas been doing?"

"Playing blackjack," Clint said.

"You?" Fortune asked.

"No, George."

"Well done, George!" Fortune said, pounding Bell on the back. "How did you do?"

"I—I—" Bell started, then swallowed and tried again. "I won."

"How much?"

"A—a hundred and twenty-five dollars."

Fortune stared at him for a moment, then looked at Clint.

"A hundred and twenty-five dollars?"

"He's overreacting a little," Clint said.

"No, no," Bell said, "you don't understand. It's not even how much I won, it's the way I won it."

"And how was that?"

Bell sat forward, warming to his subject.

"Well, I was betting five dollars at a time and, believe me, that's a lot for me."

He waited to see if Fortune would respond, and then continued when the man did not.

"Well, I was ahead fifty dollars and I wanted to stop, but Clint told me I couldn't."

"Good move," Fortune said. "When you're winning you have to push it."

Bell's eyes widened.

"That's what Clint said!"

"Good for Clint."

"But he made me bet the whole fifty dollars!"

Fortune looked at Clint and rolled his eyes.

"And what happened?"

"The dealer gave me an ace . . . uh, how do you—"

"In the hole," Clint said.

"Right, right," Bell said, "he dealt me an ace in the hole, and then he dealt me"—he paused for dramatic effect—"a king. I mean, he dealt me blackjack. Do you know how much money I got?"

"A hundred and twenty-five dollars," Fortune said.

"Right! Well, I can tell you, I was stunned. I mean . . . how did Clint know I was going to win?"

"He didn't."

"That's what I told him," Clint said.

"He just knew that you should push your luck," Fortune said.

"But . . . how do you know that? How do you know when to push your luck?"

"You just do," Fortune said. He finished his beer and sat up. "For instance, I'm going to go and push mine right now. I'll see you two later."

"Let me know when you're going to go back to your cabin," Clint said. "I want to walk with you."

"You think someone is going to try and dump me overboard?"

"You never know."

Fortune frowned, said, "Hmmmm," and then said, "Okay, I won't make a move without you."

"Good."

Fortune went off to his blackjack table, and Clint looked across the table at Bell.

"He doesn't understand," Bell said. "He bets hundreds, thousands of dollars at a time."

"He understands winning," Clint said.

"He expects to win." It sounded like a criticism.

"You should always expect to win, George," Clint said. "Expecting to lose is the wrong way to think, when you're gambling with cards, or with your life."

Bell stared at his beer mug for a few moments.

"I guess that's what's wrong with me," he said finally. "I always expect to lose."

"Why?"

He shrugged and said, "Because I always have."

"How can you say that?" Clint asked. "You have a good job, and a beautiful wife."

"I've had good things in the past," Bell said. "I always seem to mess them up, though."

"Well, maybe you'll have better luck this time," Clint said.

"Maybe."

"I think you will," Clint said.

"Why do you say that?"

"Because now you know how to push your good luck."

TWENTY-EIGHT

Bell was happy with his winnings and didn't have any desire to gamble anymore. In fact, he told Clint that he was going to go to his cabin and read.

"I'll see you in the morning," Clint said. "I should be in the dining room for breakfast no later than nine a.m."

"I'll see you there, then."

After Bell left Clint resumed his walk around the casino. It appeared they had every kind of gambling except for poker. However, Clint felt sure there was some kind of private game going on somewhere, if for no other reason than that he'd seen "Check-and-Raise" Carew on board.

Speaking of Chance Carew, Clint looked around and didn't see the man anywhere. Considering the redhead he was with, though, he might still be otherwise occupied. As far as gambling went, the night was still young.

Clint was watching a blackjack dealer who he thought might be cheating when he caught sight of a man on the other side of the room. He could actually see the man's face over the dealer's shoulder, and it took a moment for him to place him. It was the man who had been standing at the door when Gloria Aldred left. For a moment it looked to Clint as if the man was watching him, but he couldn't be sure. He decided to try to find out.

He drifted away from the blackjack tables, kept walking until he could turn around and start back, but on the other side of the tables. When he got there, though, the man was gone.

"Hi!"

He turned and saw Heather McKay looking up at him.

"Get your story in?"

"Yup," she said. "Now I'm in the mood for some gambling."

"Well, there's plenty of it here." He was still looking around for the man.

"There's only one problem."

"What's that?"

"I've never gambled."

He looked at her then and saw that she was looking at him expectantly, waiting for him to offer to teach her.

He thought, Well, why not? After all, she was a much prettier pupil than George Bell was.

"How much do you want to risk?" he asked.

"Not a lot."

"I've got just the thing for you."

He took her arm and led her over to the roulette table.

"Roulette, right?" she asked.

"Very good."

"I've heard about it, but I really don't know the rules very well."

"It's simple," he said, "and we can make it even simpler by ignoring all of the bets except the direct bets. You pick a number, put your chip on it, and if it comes up you get back thirty-five dollars for every dollar you bet."

"That much?" she asked. "Where do I get the chips?"

"How many do you want?"

"Are they one-dollar chips?"

"They can be."

"Then I think I'll take . . . ten!"

Fine, he thought, another big spender.

Clint took her money and exchanged it into chips, stacking them in front of her.

"Pick a number," he said, "and put your chip on it."

"Um . . ." She stood there with the chip in her hand, eyeing the board, while the ball started rolling.

"You'll have to do it soon," he said, "or wait until he rolls the ball again."

"Okay, okay," she said, "um, thirty-five."

"Put the chip on it."

"Oh, somebody's chip is already there."

"You can put yours on top of that bet."

"No, no, I want my own number."

"Hurry," he warned.

She leaned over, placed her chip on "34," and then straightened up. "There!"

"No more bets!" the dealer said.

"Do I have to take it back?" Heather asked.

"No," Clint said, "you got it down in time. Watch the wheel."

She did so and said, "Wow, it's hard to follow the ball."

"Don't try," he said, "just watch where it lands."

"Okay."

They both watched as the ball circled the wheel, then fell into it, bounced around from number to number before landing and sticking on number "34."

"Thirty-four," the dealer called.

"Is that mine?" Heather asked.

"It's yours," Clint said, shaking his head at her beginner's luck.

He had only begun to shake his head.

TWENTY-NINE

Heather decided to keep her chips played separate from her chips won. When she raked in her first thirty-five-dollar win she stacked it on one side, along with the original chip played. With thirty-six dollars in that stack she played another chip, leaving her with eight left to play.

She played a different number the second time and lost. She then decided that she should have stuck with number "34" so she played it again . . . and won again.

That gave her seventy-two dollars in chips on her winning side. She took another chip from her stack of seven remaining to be played and put it on "34" again.

She lost.

With six chips left to play she thought long and hard about a new number, then decided to play her age.

"25."

And won.

With five chips left to play, she had a hundred and eight dollars worth of chips won.

Clint was still shaking his head.

"What are you going to do now?" he asked.

People around the table seemed interested in that question, also. She'd won on her first, third, and fifth chip played. They were waiting to see where she was going to play her sixth.

"I think I'll stay with twenty-five," she said and put her chip there.

Clint decided that if there was a chip won and chip lost pattern, he might risk some money himself. He watched with interest as the wheel was turned, and the white ball fell on the number "1."

"One," she said, "why didn't I think of that?"

Four chips left, so she placed one on the number "1."

"You sure you want to do that?" a man standing on her left asked.

"I'm allowed to do that, aren't I?" she asked.

"Oh, you're allowed," the man said, "but the number one just came up."

"Can't it come up twice in a row?" she asked Clint.

"Sure it can," he said.

"But the odds are against it," the man said.

"The odds," Clint said, "are the same for each turn of the wheel."

"I don't think so," the man said. He was in his thirties and had enough chips in front of him to show that he'd been winning most of the night.

Clint decided not to argue the point.

The wheel started turning and Heather picked up another chip.

"Can I bet two?" she asked Clint.

"You can bet as many as you like."

With a smug look at the man on her left she placed a second chip on top of her first one.

"Sucker bet," the man said, and spread about ten chips out on the board.

Heather leaned back and asked Clint, "Why is he playing so many numbers?"

"Because he's not as lucky as you," Clint said.

They watched as the wheel turned and the ball went around the opposite way, then fell into the wheel, bounced around, and landed on number "1."

"I won again!" Heather shouted, clapping her hands.

She raked in her seventy-two chips, adding them to her stack of one hundred and eight.

"How much do I have?" she asked Clint excitedly.

"A hundred and eighty dollars."

"Oh, my God."

The man next to her was still frowning at the board.

"You have two chips left," Clint said. "Want to play them?"

"I do," she said, "one at a time. I seem to win with every other spin."

"I've noticed."

While she chose her number for this spin Clint bought himself ten dollars worth of chips. She picked number "34" again and lost.

Number "1" came up again, but she didn't seem to notice.

"Okay," she said, holding her last chip, "this is my last one, and it's a winner."

"Where are you going to play it?" Clint asked.

"Hmmm . . ."

The man next to her was watching her, also.

"I'll take number one," she said.

"Lady, forget it," the man said.

"Why?"

"It just came up three times in a row. The odds are against it coming up again."

"My friend says the odds are the same every time," she said.

"Hey, it's your money," the man said and started spreading out his chips, ignoring the number "1."

"Number one," she said and put her chip down.

"Do you mind if I play your number?" Clint asked.

"Oh, no, please do," she said. "How much are you betting?"

"Ten dollars." Clint stacked his chips on top of hers.

The man on Heather's left gave Clint a withering look and shook his head. Clint felt that the combination of her good luck and what a fourth number "1" in a row would do to this man was too good to pass up.

The wheel started turning, and then the ball.

"Never happen," the man said.

Clint and Heather watched the wheel.

"Never happen," the man said again.

The ball slowed, then fell onto the wheel, bouncing around from number to number.

Two of the numbers the man on Heather's left played were the "00" and the "13," which happened to fall on either side of the "1." As the wheel and the ball slowed the ball seemed to fall into the "13" for the last time, but then jumped to the "00" . . .

"Ha!"

. . . but then seemed to simply dribble from the "00" into the "1" again, where it stayed.

"We won!" Heather shouted.

"Son of a bitch!" the man shouted. "Four times in a row! It ain't possible."

Clint raked in their chips, handed Heather her thirty-six, which gave her a total of two hundred and sixteen dollars.

For his own ten-dollar bet Clint had a profit of three hundred and fifty dollars.

"That's impossible." The man was still complaining. "I was winning all night, and I haven't won a thing since she came and she hits five times. And number one comes in four times in a row? Can't be."

"Luck changes," Clint said to the man, who glared at him.

"Hey, girlie, what's gonna win next, huh?" the man asked her. "Tell me."

"I don't know what's going to come in on this spin," she said, "but on the next one it's going to be number ten."

"Ten? On the next spin?"

"Uh-huh."

She looked at Clint and said, "I'm finished betting now. Where can we get our money?"

"Let's go to one of the cashiers."

They exchanged their one-dollar chips for twenty-five dollar chips so that they would be easier to carry to a cashier's cage.

As they started to walk away Clint asked, "Why did you tell him what was going to come in after he was so rude?"

She giggled and said, "I lied. It's actually going to be number thirteen."

"Sure," he said.

Although she had hit on her first, third, fifth, seventh, and ninth bets Clint put that down to the whims of the wheel. It was possible that she could make ten more bets—or a hundred—without hitting once.

If it had been Clint, of course, he would have pushed his luck. Heather had no reason to.

As far as her predicting the number that would come up on the second turn of the wheel after they left, he gave it no thought. If the man wanted to believe her and play the number she gave him—"10"—it didn't matter if she was right about "13" coming up or not. The chances were he was going to lose his money, because—for whatever reason—his luck was going in the opposite direction of hers.

They walked to a cashier's cage and redeemed their chips for cash.

"We did very well," she said as they walked away from the cage.

"Yes, we did, thanks to you," he said. "How about getting a drink in the back to celebrate?"

"All right, but don't you want to know how I picked those numbers?"

"Not really."

"Do you think it was coincidence?"

"I don't believe in coincidence."

"Then what was it?"

He smiled at her and said, "It was roulette, Heather. It was roulette."

THIRTY

They sat down with a beer for each of them and Heather asked, "What did you mean, it's roulette?"

"Just that. You never know what the roulette wheel is going to do. The same number could come up two, three times in a row—"

"Or four," she pointed out.

"Or four," he conceded, though this night was the first time he'd ever seen it happen, "and then not come up for a long time."

"But I knew which numbers were going to come up."

"On every other spin?"

She nodded.

"That's not possible, Heather."

"But I did it," she said. "I have the money to prove it. So do you."

"You were at the wheel for nine spins, Heather,"

Clint said. "Try being there for ninety. You would not hit forty-five times."

"What about what I said when we left the wheel?"

"About what?"

"About number thirteen coming up."

He shrugged.

"We weren't there," he said, "we don't know what came up."

"I do," she said, "thirteen."

"Okay," Clint said, "let's say you're right. How do you know this?"

"I've just always been able to see numbers in my head," she explained.

"For instance?"

"For instance," she said, "before I went to interview for my job with my paper—"

"Which is?"

"Oh, sorry," she said, "we never did get around to that, did we? I write for the *Baltimore Sun*."

"Okay."

"I was supposed to go for my interview on the ninth day of the month," she said, "but the day before I saw the number ten clear as day in my head."

"So you went in on the tenth?"

"Yes."

"And did you let them know you'd be missing your interview on the ninth?"

"No."

"And they hired you anyway on the tenth?"

"Yes."

Clint frowned.

"Coincidence?" she asked. "I don't think so."

"So before each spin of the wheel you did what? Closed your eyes and saw a number?"

"No," she said, "I saw a number before every *other* spin of the wheel."

"Is this something you can control?"

"No."

"Then we could go to the wheel now and you might see a number before every spin?"

"Yes."

"Or every third spin?"

"That's right."

"Or not at all?"

"That's possible, too."

"So you never know."

She shook her head.

"It might not happen again, ever?"

"I don't know," she said. "I never know."

"Close your eyes now."

She did.

"What number do you see?"

She hesitated a moment, then said, "Three," and opened her eyes.

"Three what?"

"Just three."

Clint looked around, wondering—if she was right—three what?

"Hey, lady."

They both looked up because the voice was male and sounded upset. They saw the man who had been at the roulette table storming toward them.

"Can I help you?" Heather asked.

"You told me that the number ten was gonna come up," the man said.

"So?"

"I put all of my profits on it, and it didn't come up."

"You can't blame the lady for that."

"I sure can," the man said. "I'm still not convinced that the wheel wasn't fixed for her to win."

"If you think that," Clint said, "take it up with the captain, or with whoever runs the casino."

"I'm taking it up with her," the man said. "I'd advise you to butt out."

Clint stood up immediately, and the man took a half a step back involuntarily. People around them began to notice that there was a confrontation going on.

Clint and the man regarded each other for a few moments. The man was beefy, a couple of inches shorter than Clint. He was wearing a black jacket, black pants, and a white shirt that was open at the collar. He had apparently been gambling for hours, and possibly drinking during that time. His hair was in bad need of a comb, and anyone standing within ten feet of him would have appreciated it if he took a bath.

"I think you better apologize to the lady, and then leave," Clint said.

"Hey," the man said, and it was almost a whine, "I lost all my money because of her."

"Number one, you said you lost your profits, which means you're even," Clint said. "Be happy with that. Second, nobody told you to bet the number she gave you. You asked her for a number, and that's what you got."

"How come she was winning?" the man asked.

"Because she was lucky."

"I was lucky, too, until she came along."

"You can't blame your luck, good or bad, on some-body else, friend."

"Who are you?" the man demanded. "Her husband? Boyfriend? Maybe you were in on it."

"You're getting in pretty deep, friend."

The man's anger at having lost his winnings was giving him false courage—that and whatever it was he had been drinking.

He took a step toward Clint.

"Excuse me," a man's voice said, and suddenly he was there, between them. "Can I help you gentlemen?"

"Maybe you can help this fella," Clint said. "He seems to think this young lady brought him bad luck, and he was getting belligerent about it."

"Sir?" the man said to the belligerent loser. "I'll have to ask you to leave the casino."

"Hey," the man said, "I've lost money here—"

"That's not exactly true," Clint said. "If you ask the man I believe he'll tell you he's even, at this moment."

"Is that true?" The man standing between them was wearing a tuxedo but clearly had an athletic build. "Have you broken even for the evening?"

"Well, yeah," the man said, "but I was ahead—"

Abruptly, the man in the tuxedo took the other by the elbow, a hold Clint could see was a controlling one. The belligerent man had no choice but to go along.

"I'll walk you out, sir," the man in the tuxedo said. He turned to Heather and said, "I'm sorry this happened, miss."

"That's quite all right," Heather said. "If I may, I'd

like to ask the gentleman a question before he leaves?"

"Of course."

Heather looked at the man and asked, "What number did come up when you played ten?"

Sullen and defeated, the man said, "Thirteen."

As he was led away Heather looked at Clint triumphantly.

"That doesn't prove a thing," he said to her. "What does the number three mean?"

"Three men," she said, holding up her fingers. "You, the loser, and that handsome man in the tuxedo."

"Oh, hell," Clint said, "that's just—" And he stopped short.

Still looking triumphant, Heather asked, "A coincidence?"

THIRTY-ONE

Clint remained seated with a beer while Heather excused herself.

"It's late," she said, "and I'm an early riser—usually. Thank you for the gambling lesson."

"I think it's you who gave me the lesson," he said. "Perhaps we can pursue your . . . theory again tomorrow night."

"I'd like that," she said. "Good night."

"Would you like me to walk you to your cabin?" he asked. "You are carrying a lot of money."

"I'll be fine," she assured him, and said again, "good night."

He watched her negotiate the room to the exit and leave. She was a lovely girl, and turned many of the male heads in the room.

"I thought that was you," a man's voice said from behind him.

He turned in his chair and found himself looking up at Chance Carew.

"What happened to the redhead?" Clint asked, standing up.

"Ah, I see I didn't spot you first," Carew said with a smile. "The redhead is resting comfortably, thanks. It's good to see you, Clint."

The two men shook hands.

"Have a seat, Chance," Clint said.

"I'll get myself a beer first," Carew said. "You ready for another?"

"Just about."

"Good. Be right back."

While Carew was away Clint scanned the room for faces—Fortune's, the man in the tuxedo, the man he'd thought might be watching him—but he saw none of them.

"Here we go," Carew said, returning with two mugs of beer and setting one down in front of Clint. He sat down across from him and sipped his own.

"What was the commotion about?" Carew asked.

"Commotion?"

"Mmm, a few minutes ago," Carew said. "That was how I spotted you."

"Oh, that," Clint said. "A loser was accusing a friend of mine of causing his bad luck."

"The pretty girl who left?"

"Yes."

"And did she?"

Clint thought a moment, then said, "She might have, but he was rude and deserved it."

"Here's to rude people getting what's coming to them," Carew said, and they both drank to it.

"Now maybe you'll tell me what you're doing on this ship?" Carew asked. "I'm more accustomed to seeing you in some western saloon, or maybe a Barbary Coast gambling house. What puts Clint Adams on a ship to Europe?"

"An invitation."

"From who?"

"A friend," Clint said. "Sam Fortune."

Carew looked surprised.

"You're a friend of Sam Fortune's?" he asked. "I'm impressed. What did he invite you to, if I may be so bold to ask."

Clint explained about the Orient Express, and Carew listened in rapt attention.

"Sounds like a fancy do," he said when Clint was finished.

"I guess it might be."

"Not exactly your style, is it?"

"Not usually," Clint said, "but I couldn't turn down the invitation."

"I don't blame you."

"So what are you doing here?"

Carew drank some more beer then said, "The red-head. She invited me."

"Invited?"

"Insisted, in fact, that I accompany her." He leaned forward. "She has bushels of money—of course, nothing like your friend Fortune—is that his real name, by the way?"

"It is."

"I guess he decided to live up to it."

"I'll have to ask him if that was the plan," Clint said.

"Do you know that fella you almost came to blows with?"

"No, you?"

"I think so," Carew said. "I've been on a ship or two before, and I might have seen him—or at least, somebody just like him. I'll tell you who I do know, though."

"Who?"

"The man who got between you."

"I assume he works for the shipping line. Running the casino, maybe?"

"No maybe about it," Carew said. "His name is Robert Parlan."

Clint frowned.

"I know that name, don't I?"

"You should," Carew said. "He was a gambler on the circuit for years before he got this job."

"That's right, Parlan," Clint said. "A damned good poker player, or so I heard. I never got a chance to play with him."

"And you won't."

"Why not?"

"He doesn't play anymore."

"Too bad."

"He runs a game, though."

"Is that right?"

Carew nodded.

"On this ship."

''Why doesn't that surprise me?'' Clint asked. ''I knew you wouldn't be here if there wasn't a game somewhere.''

''You want in?''

''How big is it?''

''You can handle it,'' Carew said, ''if I remember correctly.''

''When is it?''

''Later tonight. Maybe your friend Fortune might even be interested. I *know* he can handle it.''

''I'll ask him.''

''Good.''

''Who else is playing?''

''Don't know,'' Carew said after he finished his beer. ''Tonight is the first night of the game. Shall I talk to Parlan for you?''

''Sure,'' Clint said, ''why not?''

''Game starts at one a.m.,'' Carew said, standing up. ''I'll meet you here at twelve-thirty.''

''Sounds fine.''

''Good to see you again, Clint.''

Clint stood and the two men shook hands again. Carew then took the same route to the exit that Heather had, only he didn't turn nearly as many heads.

THIRTY-TWO

When Clint found Sam Fortune it was almost midnight. The railroad mogul was still pounding away at one of the blackjack tables. There was a stack of chips in front of him, but Clint had no way of knowing how much Fortune had put into his quest in the first place.

"Got a minute?" Clint asked as Fortune tossed in his cards.

"I've got two," Fortune said. He looked at the dealer and said, "I'll be back."

He stepped away from the table to hear what Clint had to say. Clint quickly told him about the poker game.

"You know this fella, Carew?"

"I do."

"And Parlan?"

"I've heard of him."

Fortune stroked his chin.

"I'd like to play, but I've still got work to do at the blackjack table."

"I'll tell Carew we won't be able to play."

"Why don't you play?"

"I didn't bring that kind of money with me, Sam."

"So? I'll stake you."

"That's generous, but—"

"Generous, nothing. I want half the winnings."

"Well," Clint said, "when you put it that way."

At twelve-thirty Clint was sitting where Chance Carew had left him.

"What's the verdict?" Carew asked.

"Fortune's still playing blackjack," Clint said, "but I'm in. Where's the game?"

"It's in a room right off the casino."

"I've got to let Fortune know where I am."

"Why?"

"It's a long story," Clint said. "Let's just say he and I are just about joined at the hip these days."

"Why does that sound to me like you're looking out for him?"

"Can I let him know?"

"Sure," Carew said. "He can even come in and get you when he's ready, and stay and watch awhile. I have to warn you, though, the game's got a time limit."

"How long?"

"Five hours. By six we all have to be gone."

"That suits me. This is all cleared with Parlan?"

"Ask him yourself," Carew said, standing up, "here he comes."

Robert Parlan joined them at their small table, and

Clint stood to be introduced and shake hands.

"It's a pleasure to meet you, Mr. Adams," Parlan said. "Now that I know who you are, I'm glad I stepped between you and Dick Welby when I did."

"That's his name?"

Parlan nodded.

"I'm afraid he doesn't win very often, so he was pretty happy to be ahead when you and Miss McKay arrived at the roulette table. He tells me she had quite a run of luck."

"She did." Clint looked at Carew. "She hit five out of nine turns of the wheel."

Carew whistled.

"The wheel was solid," Parlan said. "I checked, only because I promised Welby I would. She won fair and square."

"She was betting a dollar at a time," Clint said.

"Doesn't sound like she broke the bank," Carew said.

"Will you be joining us at the game tonight, Mr. Adams?" Parlan asked.

"I will if you'll call me Clint."

Parlan smiled.

"That's a deal. Shall we go?"

"Just give me a minute," Clint said.

He found Fortune and told him where he'd be.

"Don't leave here without me," he said.

"Count on it," Fortune said. "I want to get to that Orient Express alive."

Clint returned to where Carew and Parlan were waiting and said, "Let's play poker."

THIRTY-THREE

Four hours later Sam Fortune appeared in Clint's line of vision, just behind Chance Carew. Clint simply nodded, letting Fortune know he saw him there.

A bar was set up in the room for the players and for others not playing—like Robert Parlan—so Fortune walked over and introduced himself.

"Oh, yes, Mr. Fortune," Parlan said, shaking hands, "it's a pleasure to meet you. Harry, get Mr. Fortune a drink."

"Cognac, if you have it," Fortune said.

"Of course, sir," Harry replied, as if it were silly to think he wouldn't have it.

"It's the only thing I can drink at five in the morning, besides coffee."

"We have coffee," Harry said. "I could mix the two for you, if you like."

Fortune looked at Harry, who was in his late twenties, tall and slender, and obviously good at his job.

"That'd be great, Harry. If I owned a ship, I'd hire you away from here."

"That's kind of you to say, sir."

Armed with his coffee laced with cognac, Fortune turned to Parlan and said, "Who's who and how are they doing?"

"Well," Parlan said, "of course you know Clint. Across from him is Chance Carew."

"Should I know him?"

"Early in his career he was known as 'Check-and-Raise' Carew."

"Don't know 'im, but that's poker, isn't it?"

"Yes, it is, but he raised it to an art form. The other three players are regulars who come on this cruise often. When they do they always play. Henry Ogden to Clint's left, his money is in—"

"I know who Henry is," Fortune said. "He's making a fortune in commodities."

"I don't understand it myself, but yes, he is. To Clint's right is Douglas DeWitt—"

"Publishing," Fortune said. "Seventeen newspapers, three publishing companies, and a theater in New York, I believe."

"You're very well informed," Parlan said, impressed. "The theater deal was just completed last month."

"And the other player?"

"You should recognize him from dinner," Parlan said. "I understand you were all at the captain's table."

"Oh, yes, Kirby Aldred. He has the wife with the—"

"Yes, she does," Parlan interrupted him, "and she has the appetite to go with it. While he plays cards, she prowls the ship."

"Is that a fact?" Fortune asked. "Hey, that might give me something to do tomorrow."

"If you're interested in that sort of thing," Parlan said.

"Who's ahead, here?"

"Carew and Clint. They're the only two poker players at the table. The other three are wealthy men who like to play cards."

"Yeah, Clint's pretty good, isn't he?"

"Not in the class of the great ones," Parlan said, "like Masterson, Luke Short, Ben Thompson, and some others, but better than I ever thought. I've always heard about his reputation with a gun, but he's much more than that, isn't he?"

"He sure is."

"How did you become friends?"

"He saved my life," Fortune said. "That was good enough for me."

"I imagine it would be."

"What time are they going to play until?" Fortune asked. "I'm beat."

"Probably no more than another forty-five minutes or so."

Fortune yawned.

"Don't know if I can hold out that long. I'm gonna sit over here in the corner until they're done."

"Fine."

Fortune took his coffee to one of three tables that were set up against a wall. He sat down, and in moments was asleep, with his chin on his chest.

THIRTY-FOUR

Clint shook Fortune awake at 6:05.

"What—"

"Time to go to sleep."

Fortune straightened.

"Game over?"

"Until tonight."

"How'd you do?"

"Your half is ten thousand."

Fortune wiped his eyes.

"That's all?"

Clint shrugged.

"Toward the end I started getting bad cards."

"How'd Carew do?"

"I think he's ahead about forty thousand. The others are losers."

Fortune got to his feet and looked around. There was

no one in the room with them but the bartender, Harry.

"Want some coffee?" he asked Clint.

"I want some sleep."

"Fine with me. Let's go."

They left the room, walked through the empty casino, and out onto the deck. It was just getting light and the water was calm.

"I love the sea," Fortune said. "I should take trips like this more often."

Clint had taken three of these trips in his lifetime. Once to England, once to Australia, and once to South America. This was his fourth, and he found that he didn't love it. He missed the feeling of the ground beneath his feet, or of a horse beneath him. This just didn't feel natural to him.

They went down to the deck where their cabins were and Clint walked Fortune to his.

"What time do you want to get up?" he asked.

"I don't know," Fortune said. "I usually sleep about five hours, but I think this sea air is making me real sleepy."

"Yeah," Clint said, "that and twelve hours of black-jack. How'd you do, by the way?"

"I got hot at the end," Fortune said. "I'm up ten thousand."

"Then we had a good first day," Clint said. "We both won, and nobody tried to kill us."

Fortune made a face.

"You had to remind me of that."

"That's what I'm here for," Clint said. "Speaking of which, let me take a look in your room before you go in."

"Go ahead, but make it quick," Fortune said. "The bed is calling me."

Clint went inside, looked around, and found the room clean.

"Go ahead," he said, stepping back outside. "I'll see you later. If you get up before I do, knock on my door. I don't want you wandering the ship alone."

"Will do," Fortune said, stepping inside. "Good night."

Clint waited to hear the click of the lock on Fortune's door, then walked to his own cabin. He entered and stopped short when he saw the figure in his bed. It was a woman, that much was clear. Was it Gloria Aldred? Had she gotten tired of waiting for him to show up? No, she would have made a bigger bundle under the sheet. That left only one other woman.

He moved closer to the bed and saw that he was right. It was Heather McKay. Somehow she had gotten herself admitted to his room, probably waiting for him to return to his room after the casino. Of course, she had no way of knowing that he'd been invited to a poker game. Apparently, instead of getting tired of waiting and leaving, she'd fallen asleep.

She looked very peaceful and pretty lying there, and the way the sheet hugged her it was obvious that she was naked under the sheet. Clint was simply too tired, though, to take proper advantage of the situation, so he undressed quietly, got into bed without waking her, and promptly fell asleep.

THIRTY-FIVE

When Clint awoke he turned over gently to keep from waking Heather. He was surprised to see that she was not there. Instead, there was a note on the pillow.

Dear Clint,
    Hope you had a good evening. You missed out.
See you later . . . maybe.

Heather

Clint put his hands behind his head and wondered about the time. At that point there was a knock at the door. He got up, grabbed his gun, and walked naked to answer it.

It was Fortune, looking well rested.

"You look like shit," he said.

"I just woke up."

Fortune looked at the gun.

"You don't need that," he said. "What you need are some clothes."

"Give me ten minutes, okay?" Clint said. "I'll get dressed and we'll get something to eat."

"Hurry up, I'm hungry."

"What time is it?"

"Three p.m."

"Jesus," Clint said, rubbing his hand over his face. He couldn't remember the last time he'd slept this late, no matter what time he went to bed.

"Are you alone?" Fortune asked suddenly.

"Oh, yes," Clint said, thinking of the note on his pillow, "I'm alone. Ten minutes." He closed the door.

Baker Jack entered his boss's cabin and found the man pacing.

"One day," he said, "one day in here and I'm going stir-crazy. It has to be done today, Jack, before tonight. I need to get out of here before I can spend one more night."

"I'd rather wait until we're a few more days out," Jack said, "but you're the boss."

"That's right, I am," the other man said. "Get your men together, come up with a plan, and get Sam Fortune off this ship today."

"Yes, sir."

At lunch Fortune told Clint what Parlan had said the night before about the Aldreds. Clint, in turn, told Fortune about Gloria Aldred approaching him to go to bed with her.

"And you turned her down?"

"I don't like her," Clint said. "I told her I'd be along."

"She must be as mad as a wet hen today," Fortune said. "Maybe she needs a shoulder to cry on. See, I don't like her, either, but that won't keep me from going to bed with her."

"You can have her."

"Who have you got your eye on?" Fortune asked. "That newspaper lady? She's real pretty."

"I have the feeling that she's going to be mad at me today, too."

"Keep making women mad at you, you're gonna be a lonely man."

"I'll adjust. What are your plans for today?"

"Gambling, but that won't be until tonight. I'm going to cozy up to Mrs. Aldred, but I guess that'll have to wait until tonight, too."

"How are you going to do both?"

"Don't know," Fortune said. "I guess I'll have to figure something out, won't I?"

While they were finishing up their lunch, George Bell came into the dining room and heaved an obvious sigh of relief. He almost ran over to their table.

"There you both are!"

"Where are we supposed to be?" Fortune asked.

"I didn't know where you were, or where you were supposed to be."

"Why didn't you check our cabins?" Clint asked.

"Well . . . if you were asleep or . . . or otherwise occupied . . ."

"George," Fortune said, "you astound me."

"I do?"

"Sit down, boy, have some coffee."

"Yes, sir."

"Tell me something, George—and this is a personal question."

"Yes, sir?"

Clint wondered what Fortune was getting at but was afraid he knew. Fortune was in a particularly gregarious mood this morning—this afternoon, actually—talking about what he was going to do with Gloria Aldred, another man's wife. It was for this reason that Clint was reasonably sure that his friend was going to broach the subject of George Bell's marriage.

"Why did you marry that Denise of yours?"

"Sir?"

"I'm just curious," Fortune said. "Indulge me."

Bell thought about the question for a few seconds and then said, "I loved her. I asked her to marry me. She made me the happiest man in the world when she said yes."

"And are you keeping her happy?"

"I'm trying, sir."

Fortune leaned forward and suddenly spoke in a very fatherly tone.

"Take my advice, son," he said. "Do more than try to keep her happy, but beware."

"Beware . . . what, sir?"

"Just be alert for the signs, son," Fortune said.

Bell looked confused, turned to Clint for help.

"What signs? What is he talking about?" Bell asked.

"George, your boss is a cynical man. He doesn't trust women."

"Oh, I see," Bell said. "Well, I trust Denise, Clint."

"That's good, George," Clint said, "but just as it's bad to be too cynical, it's bad to be too trusting."

"I'm not that cynical," Fortune said.

"And maybe George isn't all that trusting, Sam."

"Yes," Bell said, "I am."

Fortune looked at Clint, who shrugged. If Fortune wanted to talk to Bell about cheating wives, he was going to have to be a lot more explicit.

"Let's take a walk," Fortune said to Clint. "See you later, George."

"B-but . . . what should I do?"

Fortune and Clint exchanged a glance, and then Clint said, "Just enjoy the trip, George. Go out and look at the water."

"Well . . . can I just come with you fellas?"

"Sure," Fortune said, "fine, come along, George."

THIRTY-SIX

Baker Jack saw Clint Adams, Sam Fortune, and Fortune's flunky leave the dining room. Behind him his two men watched, as well.

"There's three of them," Mark Leland said. "Is there supposed to be three of them?"

"The young one is a flunky," Jack said, "Fortune's assistant. He won't be a problem."

"How are we going to work this?" the other man, Frank Dean, asked.

"You two take care of Fortune," Jack said. "Whatever happens, he's the one we have to get."

"You're gonna take Adams?" Leland asked.

"That's right."

"Better you than me," Dean said.

"Where are we gonna do it?" Leland asked.

151

"Let's just keep them in our sights for a while," Baker Jack said. "The opportunity will present itself."

"What are we doing?" Bell asked.

"We're looking for somebody," Fortune said.

"Who?"

"Gloria Aldred."

"Mrs. Aldred?" Bell asked curiously. "Why?"

"Because I'm going to take her to bed tonight," Fortune said.

"To bed?"

Fortune didn't reply.

Bell looked at Clint.

"Is he serious?"

"Dead serious."

"But . . . she's married."

"Not all married women are faithful, George," Clint said.

"But—"

"If you have a problem with this, Bell, I don't want to hear it," Fortune said.

Bell looked at Clint, as if pleading with him to say something.

"The woman has made it known she's available, George," Clint said. "This is her call."

"Poor Mr. Aldred."

"Mr. Aldred cares more about gambling than he does about his wife," Clint said.

"Those poor people."

Neither Clint nor Fortune had anything to say to that.

"Hey, Clint, when we spot her you've got to pull back

some, okay? If she's mad at you I don't want her trans-
ferring it to me.''

"Why is Mrs. Aldred mad at you?" Bell asked curiously.

"Your moral friend Mr. Adams, here, wouldn't go to
bed with her last night."

"She asked you?" Bell was shocked.

"Yes."

"Clint, I'm very glad you didn't—"

"I don't like her, George," Clint said, "that's why I
refused, not from any moral standpoint."

"I see."

"She's a very unlikable woman," Clint said.

"But very attractive," Fortune said.

"Yes," Clint said.

At that point Bell looked behind him for some reason
and frowned. Were those three men following them? No,
of course not. They were all on a ship. Where else did
the three men have to go?

"Is that her?" Fortune asked, stopping in his tracks.
Clint and Bell also stopped.

"It looks like her," Clint said.

Up ahead of them Gloria Aldred was sitting in a chair,
looking out at the sky and the water. She was alone.

"Okay," Fortune said, "give me some room."

"Go ahead," Clint said. "We'll wait back here."

They watched as Fortune moved ahead to approach
Gloria Aldred.

"What if her husband comes along?" Bell asked.

Clint leaned on the railing and said, "That would just
make it interesting for Sam, George."

•   •   •

"Fortune's leaving," Leland said. "What do we do?"

"He's not leaving," Baker Jack said. "Look, he's stopping by the woman."

He was, however, twenty or so yards ahead of Adams and George Bell, the flunky. In order to get to him, though, Leland and Dean would have to pass Adams, unless there was another way . . .

Bell looked behind him again and saw that the three men had also stopped. One of them looked oddly familiar to him, but he couldn't place him.

"Clint?"

"What?"

"I think . . . I'm not sure, but there are three men behind us—"

"I know," Clint said. "I saw them."

"One of them looks familiar to me."

"To me, too," Clint said. "I saw him in the casino last night, watching me. Do you know him from the ship?"

"No," Bell said, "somewhere else . . ."

"Then it would have to be from Philadelphia," Clint said. "That means they followed us here."

"From Philadelphia?" Bell asked, surprised.

"That's right."

"Are they going to try to . . . to harm Mr. Fortune?"

"Maybe, George."

"What do we do?"

"Nothing yet," Clint said. "We don't do a thing until they do."

"We just wait?"

"That's right," Clint said, "we just wait."

THIRTY-SEVEN

"A lovely lady like you shouldn't be sitting alone," Fortune said to Gloria Aldred.

She looked up at him, frowned, and then smiled.

"Mr. Fortune, isn't it?"

"Sam," he said. "May I sit with you?"

"Of course."

He sat on the chair next to her, then leaned in closer. He could smell her perfume, and her lower lip looked good enough to bite.

"Actually," he said, deciding to be very frank, "I had more in mind than just talking to you."

"Really?" Instead of being insulted, she seemed to be amused. That's when he knew that he was going to succeed. "Like what?"

"Well," he said, "I saw your husband playing cards last night."

"Yes?"

"If you'll forgive me for saying so," Fortune said, "if I were married to a woman like you, I would not waste my time playing cards."

Now it was she who leaned closer to him, until they had their heads together like coconspirators.

"This sounds very interesting," she said in a low tone. "Tell me what you would do."

"Oh, Mrs. Aldred," he said, staring straight into her eyes, "I would much rather *show* you."

He could see that the rate of her breathing had increased. He had chosen the right approach. By making it obvious that he wanted her, he had excited her.

"W-we can't go to my cabin," she said. "It's unlikely Kirby would come there, but he might—"

"He won't come to my cabin," he said. "Shall we?"

She hesitated. It wasn't that she was unused to cheating on her husband, but she rarely—if ever—did it in broad daylight. The concept of doing that now had her very excited. She also realized that Sam Fortune was a rich and powerful man.

"It's a fine way to spend an afternoon," he said.

She wet her lips and said, "Very well. Let's go."

"They're coming this way," Bell said. "I can't believe it."

"Sam's a smooth talker," Clint said. "Keep your back to them. Maybe she won't recognize me."

As it happened, Fortune was walking to Gloria Aldred's left and she had her head turned that way as they walked past Clint and Bell. There was no chance that she'd even see Clint, let alone recognize him.

As the couple went by, Clint and Bell turned their heads to watch.

"In broad daylight," Bell said, "with another man's wife."

"Well," Clint said, "they're not going to do it on deck."

"Where are they going?"

"Probably back to Sam's cabin."

As Clint watched, he saw the three men also turned their backs to Fortune and Gloria, as if they were looking out to sea. As the couple passed them, they also turned their heads to follow their progress.

"Those three men—" Bell said.

"I know," Clint said. "George, do you have a gun?"

"No," he said. "I told you before we left Philadelphia—"

"That's right, you did," Clint said. "I could give you one."

Bell went pale.

"I'm afraid I'd hit you or Mr. Fortune, Clint," Bell said. "I'm really quite hopeless with a gun."

"Well," Clint said, patting him on the back, "maybe we won't load it."

"Huh?"

THIRTY-EIGHT

"Let's go," Clint said.

"Where?"

"We'll follow Sam and Mrs. Aldred."

"But we have to go past those three men."

"I know."

"Won't they—"

"There are too many people here," Clint said.

"Then they'll probably follow us."

"I want them to."

"But, Clint—"

"Come on, George," Clint said. "Don't argue."

Clint pushed off the rail and started the same way Fortune and the woman had gone. George hurried to walk abreast of him. As they passed the three men, they all turned their attention to the sea again.

By the time Clint and George reached Fortune's cabin,

he and Gloria Aldred had already gone inside.

"How do we know they're really inside?" Bell asked.

"Put your ear to the door."

Bell obeyed. He heard voices, then what sounded like a woman's laughter, then a short scream.

"They're in there," he said.

"I know."

"What do we do now?"

"Come with me."

Clint led Bell to his cabin, and they went inside. Once there he took the Colt New Line out from under his jacket. He'd taken to wearing one on the ship, to cover the gun.

"Here," he said, handing it to Bell.

"B-but—"

"Just take it," Clint said. "You won't have to fire it."

Bell took it gingerly.

"What will I have to do?"

"Just hold it and point it."

Bell pointed it, and Clint noticed that he had his finger outside the trigger guard.

"Put your finger on the trigger, George," Clint said. "I want you to at least look like you're going to fire it."

Bell put his finger on the trigger, looking distinctly uncomfortable.

"Good. Now you can put it down."

Relieved, Bell put the gun on a nearby table.

"What will you use?"

Clint went to the bed, where he had his gun belt hanging on the bedpost. He took the Colt from the holster and tucked it into his belt.

"I'm all set."

"What do we do now?"

"Pick up the gun and put it in your belt."

Bell did so, tucking it in front.

"No, in the back, by the small of your back."

Bell did it.

"It feels uncomfortable."

"Learn to live with it for a little while. Come on, we've got to move fast."

"Where are we going?"

"Just out of here."

They went into the hall, then moved further along. Clint was trying doors along the way.

"Those are other people's rooms," Bell said to him.

"I know that, George."

As he was trying one of the doors, it swung open and a woman stood there staring at them.

"Can I help you?" she asked. She was young and attractive, despite a nose that might have been too big. She had apparently kept a late night, and was still in her nightclothes. She was short but full-bodied, and as the two men stared at her she leaned on the door, causing her robe to fall open. The nightie beneath it showed a lot of firm cleavage. Bell's eyes were almost falling out of his head.

"Yes, we'd like to come in," Clint said.

"Both of you?"

"If you don't mind," Clint said, looking down the hall, hoping the three men would not appear yet.

"Well, what did you have in mind, boys?" she asked.

"I'm sorry," Clint said, and abruptly pushed her inside so they could enter.

THIRTY-NINE

"Hey," she complained as Clint closed the door behind him.

"I'm sorry," he said again, "but we're trying to avoid three men who are trying to kill us."

She put her hands on her hips and said, "That's a new line." She looked at Bell and smiled. "Hey, you're kind of cute, sweet lips."

"M-me?"

She looked at Clint and asked, "Is he shy?"

"Very."

She reached out and stroked Bell's cheek, and he turned bright red.

"I'll say he is," she said, laughing. She turned her attention to Clint again. "So how long do you intend to stay here?"

"Not too long, I hope," Clint said. "I'll have to keep watch at the door."

"Do you mind if I get dressed?"

"Not at all."

Clint moved to the door and opened it a crack. The woman removed her robe, showing off more skin. Her breasts were full and firm, and her shoulders were rounded, not bony. Bell couldn't help but watch, but he turned away quickly as she suddenly dropped her gown to the floor.

Clint tried not to be distracted, but her breasts were pale and round. Her thighs were also round. She was a round woman, all right, but it was in all the right places.

Bell kept his eyes averted, but he managed to see that she had lots of bushy black hair between her chunky thighs.

She turned her back to them, and they both took the opportunity to study the firm globes of her chunky butt. She raised her arms over her head to shrug into a simple dress, then turned to face them while she smoothed it down. Clint saw the amused smile on her lips and knew she'd put on the performance for them to watch. He counted them lucky that they hadn't barged in on some tight-lipped spinster who might have started screaming.

"Did you like what you saw?" she asked Bell, who turned bright red again. "You really are quite adorable, aren't you?"

"I—I don't know—" he stammered.

"Quiet," Clint said as the men came into view. "They're in the hall."

It wasn't Bell but the woman who rushed over to press up against Clint and take a look.

''My name's Michelle, by the way,'' she whispered.

''I'm Clint.''

''Who's sweet lips?''

''That's George.''

She waggled her fingers at George, who smiled and waved back. She then turned her attention to the men in the hall.

Just before they entered the hall Leland asked, ''What are we gonna do?''

''They're in their cabins,'' Baker Jack said, ''and we know what Fortune and the woman are doing.''

''Are you gonna take Adams now?'' Dean asked.

''We all are,'' Jack said. ''We'll bust into his cabin and take him first. Then we can have Fortune with no problem.''

Leland pulled a gun from his shoulder holster, and Dean did the same.

''Don't go off half-cocked,'' Baker Jack said. ''We want to fire as few shots as possible. Just follow my lead. Understand?''

Both men nodded their heads but looked nervous.

''We're not goin' in there blazin', understand?''

''We understand,'' Leland said.

Dean nodded.

''Good. Let's go.''

Baker Jack started down the hall, and the other two men followed.

FORTY

"What's happening?" Bell asked, hissing urgently.

"Quiet," Clint said.

"They're just walking down the hall," Michelle told Bell.

There was a loud noise.

"What was that?" Bell asked.

"They kicked in the door to one of the cabins," Michelle said.

"Which one?"

"Mine," Clint said.

"Why didn't we just go into mine?"

For a moment Clint didn't answer. He didn't want to admit that he hadn't thought of that, because he didn't know why he hadn't.

"They might kick yours in, too," Clint said.

"So now what do we do?"

Clint looked at him.

"I know," Bell said, "we wait."

"But not long," Clint said. "I don't think it will be long at all."

Baker Jack entered Clint's cabin first, with Leland and Dean right behind him.

"Not here," Leland said.

Baker Jack looked around the empty room and then returned his gun to his shoulder holster. All three men were equipped with shoulder harnesses and the jackets they wore to cover them, compliments of Baker Jack's boss.

"I can see that."

"Where are they?"

"Bell must have a cabin."

"Where?"

"If I know Sam Fortune," Jack said, "he put his flunky on a cheaper deck."

"So what do we do now?" Leland asked, while Dean took a look under the bed.

"Now we just go and get Sam Fortune," Baker Jack announced.

"And do what with him?" Leland asked.

Baker Jack turned and looked at the two men.

"He's going to have an accident."

"What kind?" Dean asked.

"The kind you usually see on a ship."

"I ain't never been on a ship," Leland pointed out, "so I don't know what kind you usually see."

Jack stared at the man and said, "He's going to fall overboard. Put your guns away."

Clint watched as the three men came out of his cabin. The lead man looked both ways, then moved to Fortune's cabin. Clint was about to step out into the hall when he realized that none of the three men had their guns out. Naturally, they wouldn't want to shoot Fortune in his cabin. That would bring too much unwanted attention to them. If he stepped out now, they would probably draw their guns and the shooting would bring somebody out of their cabin who might get hurt.

So Clint decided to wait, knowing he was taking a chance with Sam Fortune's life but feeling justified in his decision. He just didn't think the three men were going to try to kill the railroad mogul right here. More than likely they'd want to toss him overboard and make it seem like an accident.

"What's happening?" Bell asked, unable to see out the door with Clint and the girl standing in front of it.

"They're about to kick in Fortune's door."

"What?"

"Take it easy, sweet lips," Michelle told him.

"We've got to do something."

"We will," Clint assured him, "we will. . . ."

FORTY-ONE

Baker Jack kicked in the door, and he and his men went in quickly. They saw a lot of flesh on the bed, some of it all smooth and firm breasts and buttocks, and some of it hairy and hard.

"What the—"

Leland and Dean moved quickly to the bed. First they pulled Gloria off Fortune, pawing her breasts while doing so, and then they grabbed Fortune's arms, immobilizing him.

"Who are you?" Baker Jack asked Gloria.

Instead of being frightened she was incensed.

"How dare you? Did my husband send—"

Baker Jack slapped her once, not hard, but hard enough to get her attention. He didn't like hitting women. The blow cowed her, and she regarded him from behind her hand. With her hands held up to her face, her large breasts were plainly in view and for that moment all four men were staring at her.

"Who are you?" Baker Jack repeated finally.

"Gloria Aldred."

"Who is your husband?"

"K-Kirby Aldred."

"Is he aboard?"

Before she could answer Fortune shouted, "If he was aboard, do you think she'd be here with me?" He hoped Gloria would get the message. If her husband wasn't aboard, and they didn't have to worry about her, maybe they'd leave her alive.

"Shut up!" Jack said to him. He looked at Gloria. "Is Mr. Aldred aboard?"

"N-no."

Good girl, Fortune thought.

"What do we do with her?" Leland asked.

"I know what I'd like to do with her," Dean said.

"I don't know yet," Jack said. "Get him dressed."

Leland released Fortune's arm and withdrew his gun from his holster.

"Get dressed. If you try something, I'll shoot you in the knee."

"You might miss," Fortune said. "You better aim for the heart."

Leland laughed.

"That would be too easy, old man," he said. "The knee or the elbow wouldn't be fatal, but boy, oh, boy, would it be painful."

"Get him dressed, don't have a conversation with him," Baker Jack said.

Dean looked around, found Fortune's clothes, and

threw them to him. Dean wanted to get Fortune's penis covered, because it was starting to make him feel inadequate. He'd seen men naked before, but he'd never seen one hung like a horse.

"W-what are you going to do with me?"

Baker Jack looked Gloria Aldred up and down. For a woman in her forties she had a handsome body, still firm and smooth. He felt himself hardening and thought, *If we only had the time.*

"Get dressed," he said to her.

"But—"

"Get dressed before my men get ideas."

She looked over at Leland and Dean, both of whom were eyeing her appreciatively. Neither of them offered to give her her clothes.

She crossed her arms over her breasts, walked to her clothes, turned her back, and started to dress.

"What are we gonna do with her?" Dean asked.

"She's going to have the same accident he is," Jack said.

"There's no need for that," Fortune protested. "She's innocent here. Just some shipboard fun."

"After we toss you overboard your little shipboard fun will run right to the captain," Jack said. "We can't risk that."

"Who sent you?" Fortune demanded. "Who do you work for? Who wants to go on the Orient Express in my place this badly? Badly enough to commit murder?"

"That's not for you to know, Fortune," Jack said. "Just pull on your boots and let's go."

Fortune pulled on his boots, shaking with rage and

impotence. If he stayed alive long enough, though, he knew Clint would find him.

"All right," Leland said, "stand up."

Fortune obeyed.

"Do you have a gun in here?" Jack asked.

"No."

"Don't lie," Jack said. "If we find one I'll use it on the woman before I dump her overboard."

"No gun," Fortune said. "I can't stand guns. I'm not good with them."

Leland looked at Jack, waiting for the sign to search anyway. Baker shook his head. He believed Fortune.

"Okay," Baker said, seeing that Gloria was dressed, "let's move."

"Come on!" Clint said, suddenly opening the door.

"Are we going to stop them?" Bell asked.

"No," Clint said, "we're going to get ahead of them."

"Come back soon, sweet lips," Michelle whispered loudly to Bell as he went by. "You're cute."

Bell couldn't help feeling flattered as he and Clint sprinted past the closed door of Fortune's cabin. What would Denise think when he told her?

FORTY-TWO

Clint's abrupt decision had been to get ahead of the three men, Fortune, and Gloria instead of trying to follow them. There was too much chance of being noticed. Once they were on the deck they could split up, one ahead of them and one behind them, and tail them that way until the men found an empty spot on deck to throw Fortune and Gloria overboard from.

Clint was heaving a sigh of relief inside that there had been no shots. Fortune had played it smart. If he had fought, they'd have probably killed him, and Clint didn't know if he would have been able to live with that on his conscience. He would have been second-guessing himself for the rest of his life.

Out on deck he stopped and Bell ran into him.

"We split up here."

"Split up?" Bell's voice squeaked.

"One of us will stay ahead of them, the other behind them."

"Which one am I?"

"That will depend on which way they go, Bell. Understand?"

"Oh, oh, yes, of course."

"Don't do anything until I do," Clint cautioned him.

"How will I know—"

"You'll see when I make a move."

"And then what do I do?"

"Just come rushing in with the gun in your hand and wave it around."

"With my finger on the trigger?"

"That's right," Clint said, then added, "only don't pull it."

"Don't pull it," Bell repeated, "right."

"Go, go," Clint said. "They'll be coming up this gangway any minute."

Even as he said that he wondered if there was another gangway somewhere. What if they didn't come up this way? No, he had to continue to act on his instincts.

He turned and walked the other way.

Baker Jack pushed Fortune out onto the deck, and Gloria Aldred after him.

"Go right," he said, which sent them in the direction Clint Adams had gone.

"What if we run into somebody?" Leland asked.

"We won't," Jack said. "It's dinnertime now, and the casino is open, as well. There's an area toward the front of this ship that will be ideal."

"The foredeck," Fortune said.

"What?"

"You want us to go to the fore—"

"Fore, aft, I don't know the difference," Baker Jack said. "Just walk that way until I tell you to stop."

"Sorry you got caught up in this, Gloria," Fortune said as they were walking side by side with the three men behind them.

"So am I, Sam," she said. "At least, I'm sorry they didn't bust in an hour later."

"You're a brave woman."

"When you've been married to Kirby as long as I have," she said, "death doesn't look so bad."

"We still have time."

"For what? One last good-bye? Who are these men, anyway?"

"They work for someone who doesn't want me to reach the Orient Express."

"Is that all?" she asked. "Tell them you don't want to go."

"I think it's a little too late for that."

"I was afraid you'd say that," she said. "Sam?"

"Yeah?"

"My courage has just about reached an end." He noticed the quaver in her voice.

"Stop here," Jack ordered.

Fortune looked around and saw no one. Baker Jack was right. Most of the passengers were either at dinner or in the casino.

"Mr. Fortune," Baker Jack said, "do you want to be tossed overboard, or would you rather jump?"

"Can I have some time to think about it?"

"No," Jack said. He turned to Leland and Dean. "Throw him over first, and then her."

"Maybe we could keep her for a while?" Dean asked.

"There are plenty of women on the ship, boys," Baker Jack said, "and when this is done you'll have enough money to buy any one of them. Him first, then her."

FORTY-THREE

Clint could see George Bell from his vantage point. He only hoped that Bell could see him and that he would react. Two of the men were now struggling with Sam Fortune, trying to get him to the railing. Clint looked directly at Bell, waved his arm, and then moved forward.

"Hold it!" Clint shouted, producing his gun.

The three struggling men all stopped and looked his way. The other man looked at him, and then grabbed the woman, who had also frozen.

"Stay right there, Adams, or she dies," Baker Jack said. He looked at his men. "Throw him overboard."

"I wouldn't do that," Clint said to the three men. "You'll be dead before he hits the water."

They were unsure what to do, and in that moment Fortune broke free of them and moved a few feet away from them.

"I knew you'd show up," he said to Clint, "but what took you so long?"

"I'm here, ain't I?" Clint said. "Be grateful."

"What about me?" Gloria shouted.

"Let her go, friend."

"Not a chance. You boys, kill both of them."

The two men looked at Clint, and one of them—Leland—made a move for his gun. Clint was close enough that he simply fired one shot into the toe of the man's left boot.

"Owwwwwwwiee!" the man screamed, grabbing for his foot and hopping around on the other one.

"You," Clint said to Dean, "toss your gun over the side."

Dean obeyed.

"Now see if you can catch your friend, there, and do the same with his."

Dean went to the hopping Leland and managed to get his gun from his shoulder holster. He threw it over the side.

"You're forgetting me, Adams."

"What's your name?"

"Baker Jack."

"What the hell kind of name is—oh, forget it. Put the gun down, Mr. Jack, and let the woman go."

"Why should I?"

"Because you were covered from behind even before you grabbed her."

"I don't believe you."

"George, cock the hammer back on your gun so Mr. Jack can hear it." Clint hoped that Bell would be able to accomplish that.

He did. He cocked the hammer and Jack heard it.

"Now let the woman go."

Jack obeyed.

"Throw your gun overboard."

Before he did that, Baker Jack executed a slow, half turn and looked behind him.

"Oh, you," he said in disgust, recognizing Fortune's flunky. He pointed his gun at Bell, and a split second before Clint fired, the New Line in Bell's hand went off.

FORTY-FOUR

The inaugural Orient Express trip from Paris to Istanbul was like a Mardi Gras on wheels. Clint, Fortune, and George Bell enjoyed it immensely—especially Bell, because he got a substantial raise for saving his boss's life.

On the ship, after the shooting and after the surviving men were turned over to the captain, Bell felt guilty.

"My shot missed," he said to Clint, "I know it did. You killed that man Baker Jack."

"What does it matter?" Clint asked.

"But Mr. Fortune thinks I did it."

"Let him think so, George. Where's the harm?"

"It's dishonest."

"Are you going to call me a liar in front of Sam?"

"No, I'd never—"

"Then relax. You know what you should do?"

"What?"

"Go down and visit that Michelle. I think she really likes you."

"Do you think so?"

"Sure."

"She did have a very nice body, didn't she?"

"She had a *wonderful* body."

"B-but . . . what about Denise?"

"I think when you get home you should *tell* Denise about Michelle."

"Really?"

"Really," Clint said. "Act contrite, but make sure she knows that the woman pursued you. I think it will open up all new horizons in your marriage."

Bell seemed to be thinking about that, but he later told Clint he'd been thinking about Michelle getting undressed in front of them. That was what ultimately sent him down to her cabin, where he spent a good portion of the rest of the trip.

Clint woke in his sleeper just hours before the Express was to pull into Istanbul. They'd had little time to look at Paris, but he intended to take a good long look at this city.

Heather McKay stirred in bed next to him. He'd managed to win her over after that first night's miscommunication. They had spent most of the trip in either his cabin or hers, and on the Orient Express she had shared his sleeper because otherwise she would have had to sit up the whole way.

She opened her eyes and rolled into his arms for a waking kiss. His penis thickened and pressed against her belly. She reached between them to take it in her hands. He slid his hands behind her to cup her fine ass while their tongues clashed.

"The last night," she said.

"There's still Istanbul."

"Yes, but this was our last night in this romantic car, and this is our last morning. I want you to remember it."

"I remember the whole trip, Heather."

She grinned mischievously and said, "I'm going to make sure."

She slid beneath the covers, and he felt her hot mouth engulf his penis, taking it fully inside. She started to slide her mouth up and down on him wetly, and he moaned, letting her know that he appreciated it. Just minutes later, as he erupted, the sounds of his enjoyment were bouncing off the sides of the car. . . .

He joined Sam Fortune in his car later. Gloria Aldred had already left to rejoin her husband. A half an hour before she had been saying good-bye to Fortune in the same manner Heather had been making the morning memorable for Clint. As it turned out, almost being killed together had formed a bond between them, and Fortune was quite taken with her. Of course, the fact that she was insatiable in bed added to the relationship.

"They really do have an amazing relationship," Fortune said. "I don't think I could have that kind of marriage."

"I don't think you could have any kind of marriage," Clint said.

They looked out the window as the train rolled into

the station, and there was at least as impressive a crowd as there had been to see them off in Paris.

"Think we'll ever find out who Baker Jack was working for?" he asked Clint.

"Well, with him dead and the other two unaware who he was working for, maybe not."

"You know what? I don't care. Jack's employer can remain faceless and nameless because it doesn't matter. Whichever competitor of mine it was, they didn't succeed, and I'm here."

"Which means I held up my end of the bargain. While we're in Istanbul I'm going to take in the sights with Heather."

"Good for you."

There was a knock on the door, and George Bell came in.

"Good morning, George."

"Sir, Clint. Well, we made it."

"Yes, we did, lad," Fortune said, slapping Bell on the back. "And we did it as a team."

"Yes, sir."

"Not a concept you're very familiar with, huh, Sam?" Clint asked.

"No, I wasn't," Fortune said. "But I am now, thanks to you two." He looked at Bell. "When we get off we can send that wife of yours a telegram."

"Oh, there's no need," Bell said. "Let her worry. It'll do her some good."

"Is that old George I hear talking?" Fortune asked.

"No, sir," Bell said, "this is the new George. Things are going to change when we get back home."

"Just keep your eyes open, boy," Fortune said, "and you'll see more changes than you think."

Fortune left the cabin to get to a train exit where photographers would be waiting. As Bell and Clint followed him, Bell asked, "Now, what did he mean by that?"

"Just a little cynical advice, George," Clint said, "which I think you'd better take heed of."

Watch for

THE POSSE FROM ELSINORE

189th novel in the exciting GUNSMITH series
from Jove

Coming in September!